CASTLE OF BLOOD

WARHAMMER HORROR

• THE VAMPIRE GENEVIEVE •
by Kim Newman

DRACHENFELS
GENEVIEVE UNDEAD
BEASTS IN VELVET
SILVER NAILS

THE WICKED AND THE DAMNED
A portmanteau novel by Josh Reynolds,
Phil Kelly and David Annandale

MALEDICTIONS
An anthology by various authors

THE HOUSE OF NIGHT AND CHAIN
A novel by David Annandale

CASTLE OF BLOOD
A novel by C L Werner

THE COLONEL'S MONOGRAPH
A novella by Graham McNeill

PERDITION'S FLAME
An audio drama by Alec Worley

THE WAY OUT
An audio drama by Rachel Harrison

CASTLE OF BLOOD

C L WERNER

WARHAMMER HORROR
A BLACK LIBRARY PUBLICATION IMPRINT

First published in Great Britain in 2019 by
Black Library,
Games Workshop Ltd.,
Willow Road,
Nottingham, NG7 2WS, UK.

10 9 8 7 6 5 4 3 2 1

Produced by Games Workshop in Nottingham.
Cover illustration by Rachel Williams.

Castle of Blood © Copyright Games Workshop Limited 2019. Castle of Blood, Warhammer Horror, GW, Games Workshop, Black Library, The Horus Heresy, The Horus Heresy Eye logo, Space Marine, 40K, Warhammer, Warhammer 40,000, the 'Aquila' Double-headed Eagle logo, and all associated logos, illustrations, images, names, creatures, races, vehicles, locations, weapons, characters, and the distinctive likenesses thereof, are either ® or TM, and/or © Games Workshop Limited, variably registered around the world.
All Rights Reserved.

A CIP record for this book is available from the British Library.

ISBN 13: 978-1-78999-017-1

No part of this publication may be reproduced, stored in a retrieval system, or transmitted in any form or by any means, electronic, mechanical, photocopying, recording or otherwise, without the prior permission of the publishers.

This is a work of fiction. All the characters and events portrayed in this book are fictional, and any resemblance to real people or incidents is purely coincidental.

See Warhammer Horror on the internet at

blacklibrary.com

Find out more about Games Workshop
and the worlds of Warhammer at

games-workshop.com

Printed and bound in China.

To Jim, for braving this tome of horror in its early stages.

WARHAMMER HORROR

A dark bell tolls in the abyss.

It echoes across cold and unforgiving worlds, mourning the fate of humanity. Terror has been unleashed, and every foul creature of the night haunts the shadows. There is naught but evil here. Alien monstrosities drift in tomblike vessels. Watching. Waiting. Ravenous. Baleful magicks whisper in gloom-shrouded forests, spectres scuttle across disquiet minds. From the depths of the void to the blood-soaked earth, diabolic horrors stalk the endless night to feast upon unworthy souls.

Abandon hope. Do not trust to faith. Sacrifices burn on pyres of madness, rotting corpses stir in unquiet graves. Daemonic abominations leer with rictus grins and stare into the eyes of the accursed. And the Ruinous Gods, with indifference, look on.

This is a time of reckoning, where every mortal soul is at the mercy of the things that lurk in the dark. This is the night eternal, the province of monsters and daemons. This is Warhammer Horror. None shall escape damnation.

And so, the bell tolls on.

GUEST LIST

Count Wulfsige von Koeterberg – last of the von Koeterbergs, master of Castle Mhurghast

---

Ottokar Hausler – swordsmith

    Inge Hausler – his wife

    Magda Hausler – their daughter

Lothar Krebs – alchemist

    Saskia Krebs – his wife

    Thilo Krebs – their son

Hartmann Senf – merchant

    Sigune Senf – his wife

    Heimo Senf – their son

    Herlinde Senf – their daughter

Notker Volkeuhn – former priest

    Ludgera Volkeuhn – his wife

    Reiner Volkeuhn – their son

Bruno Walkenhorst – merchant, veteran Freeguild officer

    Bernger Walkenhorst – his son

Baroness Hiltrude von Woernhoer – noblewoman

    Baron Roald von Woernhoer – her husband

    Liebgarde von Woernhoer – their daughter

Nushala Iliviar – aelf scholar

    Abarahm Iliviar – her son

Alrik Blackthumb – duardin cogsmith

    Brond Alriksson – his son

PROLOGUE

Darkness, heavy and dank, infested the cellar. The blackness stretched across the ceiling, sprawled along the floor, clung to the walls in a thick skein of brooding shadows. The air itself was rank with the absence of light, cold and clammy as it was drawn with each breath. There was an atmosphere of lurking menace, the nameless fear that plucks at the heart when midnight crawls across the land.

The old man's wrinkled hand closed tighter about the ivory walking stick he held. His bleary eyes stared into the darkness, instinct defying the logic that told him he could see nothing. His ears strained for every sound. He could hear the creep of centipedes as they stalked rats in the dark. The drip of water falling to the cellar floor. The rasp of gnawing fangs as vermin tried to chew their way into boxes and barrels. There was nothing to betray the presence of someone waiting in the room. Just the same, the old man knew it was not empty.

'He is here?' he whispered, his lisp drawing out the words.

'He's here,' confirmed the trader who stood just behind the old man on the copper stairs. He drew a long rod of alabaster from his belt and set his palms against either end of it. The middle of the rod began to glow, throwing a bluish light across the cellar.

The cellar was a large room, with walls fashioned from blocks of dark iron. The floor was dirt and sparkled with the copper flecks mixed into its grains. Heavy archways supported the high ceiling and the bronze-sheeted roof. Much of the room was occupied by tin boxes and bronze barrels. Rats and centipedes alike retreated from the light.

There was one occupant of the cellar who did not retreat. He rose from the crate he had been sitting on when the trader activated his torch. He was so tall that he seemed almost like an ogor from the savage wilds – and such a comparison was not unjustified. His was a barbarous aspect. His dark skin was tattooed in white, creating a deathly image. His face was stained, teeth inked across his lips, his eyes staring from the sockets of a painted skull. Each bone was picked out in white on his long fingers and brawny arms. He wore a morbid helm fashioned from the head of a wolf, its snout and fangs stretching across his forehead. A breastplate of assorted bones was tied around his chest. A short skirt of skin circled his waist, the withered face of the man whose body had been flayed to craft the garment frozen in a silent scream.

'This is him,' the trader said, not without a shudder.

The old man limped down the last few steps, leaning heavily on his stick. He knew he was a complete contrast to the barbarian. His body was frail, wasted and thin beneath the velvet coat he wore. Frilled cuffs fell around his shrivelled hands, and rings of teak and mahogany circled his fingers. The buttons on his vest were of pure ebony, and the buckle on his belt was of polished cherrywood. There was the smell of rosewater on his pale, wrinkled skin. Nothing, however, bespoke the great wealth he enjoyed like the gold-petalled lily that was pinned over his heart. Scarce was the soil vibrant enough to support such delicate growth in this region of Chamon.

'This is him,' he repeated as he walked down to the cellar. There was no trepidation in his voice, only eagerness.

The trader stepped down to accompany the old man. He was middle-aged, his brown hair rapidly retreating from the middle of his head, silver sneaking into his thick moustache. His build was heavy, straying towards a paunch. His crimson doublet was not so refined as the coat of his companion, but there was a gaudy opulence in its flash of embroidered vines and leaves. Everything in his garb was of a similar character, loudly announcing prosperity and lacking the refinement of the old man's riches. For the trader, wealth was an accomplishment to be boldly proclaimed. To the old man it was a natural birthright.

'Thokmal has journeyed far to bring what you seek, Your Illustrious Highness,' the trader said. He gave the old man an apologetic look. 'I'm afraid that the expense I've incurred is more than we originally bargained.'

The old man fixed the trader with a steely gaze. 'You will be paid, Gustav.' He reached for his belt and untied the leather bag hanging there. Turning his attention back to the barbarian, he tossed the pouch to Gustav. 'Money is of little value to me now.'

Gustav pounced on the bag and quickly opened it. He grinned as he filled his fist with teakwood coins.

'Take whatever you need for your commission,' the old man said as he walked towards the barbarian. 'How much do you want?' he asked the tattooed tribesman.

Thokmal crossed his brawny arms and returned the old

man's gaze. The barbarian's eyes were intense, the pupils tinged a raw and vicious red. The stare of the wolf whose head he wore could not have been more ferocious. The old man could feel the hate, the smouldering rage behind the tribesman's eyes. The bloodlust just waiting to be unleashed.

'No money,' Thokmal said at last. His voice was a deep rumble, like the pulse of a war drum. 'You cannot buy what I have brought.'

The old man reared up, the ivory stick raised to strike Thokmal. 'You have brought it and it will be mine!' he hissed. His aged frame trembled with fury.

'You cannot buy what I have brought,' the barbarian repeated. His face pulled back in a cold smile, his real teeth showing beneath those inked across his lips. 'It can only be given.'

'Given?' the old man muttered, his arm still raised to strike.

Thokmal nodded. 'I do not sell.' He pointed at Gustav, crouched on the floor counting his coins. 'He would sell it. I will not.'

'Then I will take it!' the old man snarled. The ivory stick swung down at Thokmal's head. The barbarian caught it in his hand and plucked it from the old man's grasp as though he were but a child. The old man staggered, almost falling onto the floor as he lost his balance. He managed to keep from collapsing by sheer force of will. He would not prostrate himself before a savage from the wilds.

'You understand,' Thokmal growled, approval in his tone. 'You know what it is you ask for. What it means. How it must be used.' The barbarian tossed the ivory stick back to the old man. 'I see in your eyes the same fire that is in mine. You know how it must be used. And you will use it.'

'It will be used,' the old man hissed as he leaned against his stick once more. 'It will be used more than even your bloodthirsty soul would dare!'

'There is a price,' Thokmal warned.

'And I will pay it,' the old man said. 'Gladly. Happily. I have waited twenty years, and now what I want is within my grasp!' His face darkened. 'Give it to me, or I will take it from you.'

The barbarian glared back at the old man. 'It does not matter from whence the blood flows,' he growled.

'But your god does care how much blood is given to him,' the old man retorted. 'Yes, you can kill me, but I promise you that in doing so you will be cheating your god. Give it to me and your god shall have a feast. I will give him gallons of blood! Pools of it!'

Thokmal again held the old man's gaze. Slowly he reached for a bundle of skins resting on the box beside him. His stained fingers pulled away the dried gut that bound the bundle together. As he drew the covering back, a sinister object was revealed. It was a long knife of bronze, its blade curved like a sabretusk's claw, its pommel shaped into a skeletal visage. An air of evil radiated from the weapon, a miasma of murder and massacre.

The old man hurried forwards, ignoring the pain in his aged bones. His lips curled in a triumphant smile. 'At last revenge will be mine,' he chortled.

The barbarian took a step back and studied the old man. Thokmal was pleased by what he saw.

'You see, Your Illustrious Highness,' Gustav crowed from back near the stairs. 'I told you he'd bring the phurba.' He pointed at the sinister knife Thokmal had revealed. 'All I had to do was let the Skullcaller tribe know you were seeking it.

The old man turned and fixed Gustav with a grim look. 'And now you know that I have found it.'

Gustav cringed at the murderous tone in his patron's voice. 'We... had... an agreement,' he sputtered as he stumbled to his feet, his hands closing tight around the money.

'You were paid,' the old man sneered. His eyes glittered with malice. 'I can trust you to bring me something for pay, Gustav, but how can I ever trust you to keep quiet about what I have bought?'

'You can trust me! You can trust me!' the trader insisted as he slowly backed away towards the steps.

The old man shook his head. 'A man who values only money can never be trusted.' He looked aside, at Thokmal. 'I have only just met your friend, but we understand each other better than you can imagine.'

Gustav cried out and turned to run. Thokmal's hand had darted for the bone vest he wore. Before the trader could reach the bottom step, his cry of fear became a groan of agony. A bone-handled knife shivered in the middle of his back, thrown across the cellar by Thokmal. The tribesman stalked over to Gustav and ripped the blade free. Coldly, he flipped the wounded man over and plunged the knife into his heart.

The old man paid no notice to Gustav's murder. He was too busy winding the skin coverings back around the phurba. He held the bundle close to his chest as he limped across the cellar.

'I will know if you do not use it,' Thokmal warned as the old man walked past him.

'You can leave Gustav's body here when you are through,' the old man said. 'This is where he hid contraband. None of his serfs know about this place. Nobody will find him.'

Thokmal twisted his knife, cracking Gustav's ribs. He reached into the trader's chest and pulled out the dripping heart. He shook the disembodied organ at the old man. 'You have made a promise to my god. Khorne will be angry if you break your oath.'

The old man laughed, a sound as cold as the hiss of a serpent. 'I have waited twenty years for this. No power of gods or men will keep me from my revenge.' He studied Thokmal for a moment. He was pleased by the uneasiness he saw when the barbarian met his gaze.

'I believe you,' Thokmal said. 'I think I will leave this place as quickly as I can. I will return to my tribe.' His smile was as cruel as it was nervous. 'I believe your words, and I know the carnage that will spawn from them.'

The old man turned away and started up the steps. 'Yes,' he muttered. 'Death now walks the streets of Ravensbach.'

CHAPTER I

Magda brought the slim, rakish blade whipping around. The sword slashed across its target, ripping deep into the bloated paunch. Innards spilled out and streamed across the copper-sheeted floor. A smirk of satisfaction teased at the young woman's lips. She quickly tried to correct herself and adopt a more sombre pose, but she already knew it was too late. She had exposed herself and would now suffer the price.

'A lack of focus will get you killed.' The scolding words rang across the room.

Magda turned around and sheathed her sword. She set her hands on her hips and threw back her head in an effort to look defiant. Inside, though, she felt as if a bunch of mice were running around her guts. However hard she worked, however independent she thought herself, the displeasure of her father made her feel like a guilty little girl caught swiping fruit from the larder.

Ottokar Hausler stamped his way across his shop, each step

a little heavier than the last. He used his left hand to brush away the belts and scabbards that hung from the beams. The right did not so much as sway as he walked, locked in place at his side. A dark glove covered the right hand, and the sleeve of his doublet covered almost all of the rest. There was only a little patch behind the wrist that was uncovered, revealing a flash of silver.

'You have to concentrate,' Ottokar said. His face was full, just on the verge of becoming flabby. The sharp nose was tinged red and the cheeks were flushed. There was still a keenness in his eyes, but it was dulled by the sheen of liquor. The sound of swordplay could still rouse him from his cups.

Magda swept a stray lock of night-black hair from her face and matched her father's judgemental stare. She pointed to the stuffed target dummy she had disembowelled, sand still running from it onto the floor. Unlike her father's, the glove she wore was to better her grip on a sword, not hide an infirmity. 'My technique improves every day,' she proclaimed. 'I'm faster and more accurate–'

Ottokar waved aside her boast. 'Skill is not enough,' he said. 'Discipline! Discipline is the key. You can be fast as lightning, precise as a viper, but still be an amateur with the sword.' He came a few steps closer and then stamped his foot down on the pedal that controlled the target dummy.

Magda whipped around, and the blade leapt from its scabbard and ripped across the throat of the sackcloth dummy. More sand rained down on the floor. She started to turn back to her father. Only then did she realise he had stamped on the pedal a second time. The dummy was swinging around, a wooden sword in each of its eight arms. There was no time for her to dart in and strike, and no chance to parry all of the enemy swords. She jumped back and crashed to the floor.

'Never let down your guard,' Ottokar warned.

'My blade crossed its throat,' Magda countered. 'If it had been a man, he would be dead.' She rose to her feet and started brushing dust from her breeches.

Ottokar shook his head. 'Some men take more killing than others, and the dead do not stay as dead as they should be.' He sighed and gave her a studious look. 'I would think that your paramour would have told you something about those kinds of things.'

It was one barb too many for Magda. Perhaps he was justified in criticising her ability with the sword, but he had no authority to speak about anything else she did. Ottokar had forfeited that right a long time ago.

'You surprise me, father. You condescended to take an interest in me.' Magda recovered her sword from the floor and swept it through the empty air. 'Aside from what I can do with this.'

The sharp words caused Ottokar to look away. He glanced across his workshop, at the swords hanging on the walls and resting in barrels. The forge and the anvil, the ingots of bronze and iron and steel that he would shape into weapons. In one corner, each perched on its own stand, were elegant blades crafted in another time, weapons Ottokar would not allow anyone to buy. They had to be earned, bestowed on those the swordsmith felt were worthy of them. Guilt gnawed at Magda when she reflected that she was one of the few to have been given one of those swords.

'This is my world,' Ottokar said. 'This is the only place where I am any good to anyone.' He reached over with his left hand and gripped the lifeless hulk that had replaced his right. The motion caused anger to swell within his daughter.

'Spare me the melancholy,' Magda snapped. 'You lost your arm in a duel, not your life.'

Ottokar looked at her, his eyes glittering with emotion. 'Were they not the same thing?'

'Only for someone who cares only about swords,' Magda retorted.

'You were too young to remember...'

'Yes, I was too young to know who you were before you lost your arm. That's an excuse I have heard many times, father. I weary of hearing it.' Magda slammed the sword back into its sheath and marched towards the shop's exit. 'Do one thing for me,' she said as she passed Ottokar. 'Wait until I've left before you crawl back into the bottle.'

Magda could hear her father stamping his way across the workshop while she climbed the stairs that led up to the family's home above the business. Briefly she thought about going back and apologising for her harsh words. She discarded the idea. She didn't have anything to apologise for.

She brushed aside the strings of polished tin that curtained off the entranceway and stepped into the little courtyard beyond. Water bubbled from the bronze fountain that loomed over the little pool in the middle of the area. Imitation trees with fronds of painted electrum cast shade over the courtyard. Stone benches were scattered about in the shadows. A few marble-coloured birds flittered about, tweeting at each other with shrill cries. They scattered as Magda walked towards the curtained doorways at the far end of the courtyard.

A strong smell of boiling stew struck her nose as she stepped into a long common room. Magda looked towards the doorway leading into the kitchen. She could hear the sound of plates and bowls being moved around. A moment later her mother emerged from behind the curtain of tin strings.

Inge Hausler was not quite twenty years older than Magda, but age had touched her so softly that they might pass for sisters. She was not quite as trim and fit as her daughter, her long legs lacking the corded muscles of her child's, her arms devoid of the strength that characterised the swordswoman.

But her face had that same classic loveliness – big blue eyes and high cheek bones, a soft snip of a nose and lush full lips. Inge kept her raven tresses loose and wild, a dark cascade that spilled down her shoulders and across her breast. Magda preferred to keep her own hair tied back so that it would not be in the way, but her mother seemed to delight in the disordered abandon of her own. She was often trying to get Magda to follow her example.

Inge smiled. 'Sounds like practice is over for today.' She wiped her hands on the apron she wore over her jade-coloured dress. She arched an eyebrow when she noted Magda's demeanour. 'I take it you two had words again. The miserable sot should know better when to keep his tongue in a bottle.'

As angry as she was, Magda took offence at the disparagement of her father. Even if her mother was voicing her own thoughts of only a moment before. 'He means well,' she said. 'It's hard on him. A swordsmith with only one arm. He has to leave most of the work to his apprentice and put his stamp on blades he feels are beneath his quality. That can't be easy for him.'

'Ottokar never chose anything that was easy,' Inge said acidly. 'Always had to keep proving himself. Never knew when something was good enough. Could never be satisfied to leave things as they were.' She shook her head and gave Magda an excited look. 'You'll never guess what happened today. A messenger came from Count Wulfsige von Koeterberg!'

Magda gave her mother a puzzled stare. 'The count? What could he want with us?'

Inge bristled at the incredulous tone. She puffed herself out, taking on the arrogant air she always adopted whenever someone questioned her status. 'I'll have you know that we've been invited to dinner at Mhurghast Castle. All of us are to be Count Wulfsige's guests.' She tossed her head back, the long raven tresses sweeping around her like the waves of some black ocean. 'There was a time when I was courted by the count's son. If things had turned out differently, you might have been a nobleman's daughter instead of a drunkard's.'

'But why does the count wish to entertain us?' Magda pressed. 'I don't understand.'

Inge frowned and stepped back into the kitchen. A moment later she came out with a thin sheet of copper, upon which had been etched the invitation. Affixed to the bottom of the metal page was the wax seal of von Koeterberg, a castle flanked by lightning bolts. 'Here, since you seem to think I am making things up.'

Magda read the invitation. It was just as her mother said, but that only raised more questions. 'But why?'

'When good things happen, accept them,' Inge advised her. 'Count Wulfsige is one of the wealthiest men in Ravensbach. Can you imagine the spread he'll have!' She glanced back at the kitchen and frowned. 'At least for one night there won't be squab stew and beans. We'll eat like ladies and lords should.'

'The invitation only says to bring the family,' Magda said, reading the page. 'There's no mention of how many. Do you think it would be all right to ask Klueger to come?'

Inge sighed in exasperation. 'That man is beneath you,' she said. 'You're a beautiful girl. You can do much better than him.'

Colour rushed into Magda's cheeks. First the old argument with her father, now the ongoing one with her mother. 'I don't care about better. I love Klueger.'

'Love.' Inge tutted and shook her head. 'How long do you think that will last? The man's prospects are limited. What kind of advancement does he have with those Sigmarite priests?' She looked at the room around them and frowned.

'Even the best of them couldn't afford this. You'd be stepping down, not up.'

'We aren't having this discussion,' Magda stated.

'I'm only looking out for what is best for you,' Inge replied. 'You're still young. You could have any man you turned your attention to. I don't want you to waste your opportunities the way I did.'

Magda's hands curled into fists at her sides. Before she could think, the words were spoken. 'I'm not sure you wasted any opportunity, mother.'

Inge's eyes went wide with shock. She snatched the invitation from Magda's hand with such force that it sliced her palm. 'The messenger said to bring my family,' she said as she turned and walked back into the kitchen. 'That man is not part of my family, and he never will be.'

Magda stared after her mother as the tin strings fell back into place. She truly regretted the horrible thing she had said. She knew her mother loved her deeply and was only trying to do what she thought was best. The problem was that what was smart wasn't always what was right. Magda trusted her feelings more than her mother's strategising.

Blood dripped from the cut on Magda's hand. She glanced down at it and the now ruined glove. More than her injury, she was thinking about the invitation.

They never did decide why Count Wulfsige should ask them to dinner at the castle.

Bruno Walkenhorst was rummaging in the old iron chest. He couldn't remember the last time he'd even opened it. Was it ten years ago, or only five? It had been a long time, in any event. So long that as he shifted the contents around, the old cloaks and threadbare hats, he started to wonder if what he was looking for was even there. Maybe he'd got rid of it some time back. It was possible his wife had thrown it out. She had always been avid about getting rid of what she termed clutter.

Bruno paused in his rummaging. A maudlin look fell across his weather-bitten face. Kirsa. It was seven years since she'd died… No, if he was going to be honest with himself, he had to face it. Kirsa had been murdered, stabbed by men who mistook her for him in the dark. Bruno had paid back that debt of blood, but it did little to ease the pain of her loss. After all these years, just thinking about her made his heart feel like a slab of ice.

He'd quit the business after that. It was ironic that he still thought of it as his 'real' business, even though he had been legitimate ever since Kirsa's death. Bruno couldn't quite think of himself as a merchant, a humble seller of whatever goods he could secure at a discount. He still thought of it as a front for the merchandise he'd once smuggled into Ravensbach or the stolen goods he'd fenced for thieves and burglars. Unhealthy people to know, smugglers and thieves, but then, they weren't always that way. Not at the start.

A flash of gold at the bottom of the box caused Bruno to search faster. He pushed aside the accumulated bric-a-brac and uncovered what he'd been looking for. He lifted the tunic out of the box and unfolded it. The once vibrant blue had faded considerably over the years, but the brass buttons and golden braid were still as smart as the first day he'd worn it. He held the coat against his chest and tried to estimate how it would fit. There might be some trouble getting it buttoned up, but that was to be expected after almost twenty years.

So many years. So much time since he'd been the dashing young captain in the Freeguild. Bruno had led men into the wilds of Chamon, pushing back against the savagery that threatened Ravensbach. They had battled orruks and beastkin, grot raiders and human barbarians. Whatever the enemy, the Ravensbach Freeguild had marched forth to send them back into the wastelands. It was by their efforts that the city had been able to expand, to establish new mines and farms, maintain the trade routes that allowed it to flourish.

Bruno sifted through the box and withdrew the cocked hat that accompanied the jacket. Stark white once, it had darkened to a musty grey. The brilliant plume that had been pinned to its side was only a tattered memory now, a raw quill with a few frayed specks of feather. He smiled as he remembered all the trouble the plumes had given him. They became so worn out that he always had to keep a few replacements with him on campaign. He groped around the box until his hand came upon a little bronze case. Lifting it out, he snapped it open and was rewarded with the sight of a long red feather. He'd be able to replace that shabby veteran after all.

'Father, are you up there?'

The voice came from the apartment below. Bruno gathered up his mementos of the past and started down from the attic. The iron ladder trembled as he stepped down its rungs.

Waiting below was a young man with sandy-brown hair and a muscular build. His tunic was rough leather, his belt made from the scaly skin of a copper-throat. His breeches were a dun colour, woven from the tough fibres of the web-weed. It was the boots, however, that drew Bruno's attention. They were high and stiff, rising almost to the knees, made of ox hide and stained a dark black. Except, of course, for those spots that were spattered with dun-coloured mud.

'You've been out with that gang again,' Bruno grumbled as he stepped down into the apartment. The common room was large enough, and appointed in a lavish if outdated style. He'd always done his best to indulge Kirsa, but he'd seen no reason to indulge himself when she was gone. As for their son... Bruno wondered if he'd indulged the boy too much.

'That gang, as you call them, are my friends,' the youth said, annoyance in his voice.

'Bernger, having the wrong friends is worse than no friends at all,' Bruno said. 'You have to recognise when they've gone bad, so that you don't go bad too.'

'There's nothing–'

Bruno cut him off. 'How much did you steal this time? And from who?' He scowled and walked over to the copper-faced liquor cabinet. 'Never mind. I know you won't tell me anyway. You're young enough to still believe in honour among thieves.' He poured himself a glass of brandy.

'It isn't as bad as you always think,' Bernger explained. 'We only take from those who deserve to be robbed.'

Bruno sank back in a chair, the coat and hat sprawled across his lap. He stared up at his son. 'That's how it always is. How it always starts. Someone you don't like has too much, so you take it from him. Somebody you feel is cruel or unjust happens to be rich, so you steal some of it.'

'I understand you got your start when you stole provisions from the Freeguild,' Bernger reminded his father.

'You must've been speaking with Romauld,' Bruno said. 'Maybe Markolf. I'm surprised you've been chatting with their sort. But then I suppose you need someone to fence your goods.'

Bernger frowned at the disdain in his father's eyes. 'Are those stories wrong?' he challenged.

Bruno took a slow sip of brandy. 'No,' he confessed. 'That's how it started. Romauld, Markolf...' He paused, not wanting to speak the names of the men who had murdered Bruno's mother. 'A few others. We took bread and meat from the storehouse. There was a famine in Ravensbach. The only people who had enough to fill their bellies were the nobles and the soldiers. That wasn't right, so we decided to redistribute the food among our families and friends.' He again paused, and gave Bernger a hard look. 'That's how it starts. Noble ideas and good intentions. But it doesn't stay that way. You toss aside honour for necessity. Then the next time you need even less reason to steal. So it goes on and on, until you're right down in the gutter with the rats.'

'It isn't like that,' Bernger objected. 'We only take–'

'From bad people, I know,' Bruno interjected. 'And one day, all it'll need to make someone bad is simply that they have something you want.'

'You don't understand.'

'Better than you imagine.' Bruno gulped down the rest of the brandy. 'I see so much of myself in you, it's almost painful. Don't make the same mistakes I made, boy. Keep your head high and your hands clean.'

Bernger shook his head. 'I need to make my own way. I want to make something for myself. I don't want to just hang around like a vulture waiting for my inheritance. You've given me a lot, done everything you could for me, but I've got to do something for myself. I've got to do it on my own.'

'By stealing?'

'That's how you got your start,' Bernger retorted.

It took some time for Bruno to reply. It wasn't anger that kept him silent. It was guilt and shame and pain and regret, all melded into one sickening sensation. 'I did it wrong,' he finally said. 'I tried to find a shortcut, but there are no shortcuts. Everything has its price. Some prices are too dire, but you don't always know what you're paying until it's too late.'

Bernger was quiet for a time, his emotions hard to read. When he did speak, it was to change their discussion entirely. He pointed at the coat and hat resting in Bruno's lap. 'What made you dig those old rags out?'

'I'll thank you not to call my uniform "old rags",' Bruno

chided. He stood up and put the hat on his head, then smoothed out the coat and threw it over his shoulders.

'You understand that's never going to fit you,' Bernger said.

Bruno frowned. 'I just need to stuff myself into this coat for one night. That's all I ask of it.'

A puzzled look came across Bernger's face. 'One night? What is this all about?'

Chuckling, Bruno walked over to the silver-ornamented table that stood near the entryway. He picked up the copper sheet that was resting there and held it out to his son. 'An invitation,' he said. 'You and I have been invited to dinner at Castle Mhurghast by Count Wulfsige.'

Bernger's bewilderment only increased as he looked over the message. 'Why would the count invite us? We're hardly of a station to warrant such notice.'

There was a wistful tone in Bruno's voice when he answered. 'That's why I dug out the uniform. A long time ago, when I was a captain in the Freeguild, I was a friend of the count's son, Hagen. I think he's feeling nostalgic for old times. The count must be nearing ninety. He probably wants to see people who will remind him of happier times. Rekindle old memories.'

Bernger glanced down at his clothes. 'If we're visiting the count, I'll have to get something suitable for the occasion. I don't want to be mistaken for a servant.'

A bitter memory stirred at the back of Bruno's mind. 'I shouldn't worry,' he said. 'To Count Wulfsige, there isn't a soul in Ravensbach he regards as anything more than a servant.'

The steps of Baron Roald von Woernhoer echoed through the hall. A servant in white livery hurried behind the noble, wiping the marks of his boots from the marble floor. The hallway, with its limestone pillars and oak ceiling, was a display of opulence and wealth few in Ravensbach could match. Roald was fanatical about maintaining the immaculate condition of this extravagance. No one, even other nobles, was allowed to walk across the polished marble without first putting silk slippers on their feet. The lamps that hung from the ceiling were lit by elaborate devices of duardin manufacture rather than anything that might drop wax or exude smoke. The limestone pillars were coated in a special unguent, an alchemical sheen that prevented fingers from leaving a mark upon them. The doors that opened into the hallway were fashioned from cherrywood and pine, beech and alder, their latches and handles sculpted from lapis lazuli and pearl.

There could be no greater evidence of the excitement the message had raised in the baron than that he should forego every rule of his household and march through the hall with his boots on. His customarily stern visage was lit by an almost palpable eagerness. In a low whisper he muttered a single word to himself as he stalked down the hall.

'Finally.' Roald rolled the word over his tongue, savouring it like a choice delicacy. He clenched his fingers tight around the copper sheet, as though afraid it would vanish if he lost his grip on it. When his steps carried him to an elaborately carved cherrywood door, his eyes focused on the images of dragons and gods. Sigmar and Dracothion, repeated in different poses on each panel. He had paid a small fortune for that artistry, a gesture meant to impress Ravensbach's lector. Well, it seemed he would no longer have to impress anybody in the city. Not any more.

'Open it,' Roald snapped at the servant who had followed him down the hall. The menial scrambled forwards and pushed the portal inwards. The baron quickly followed him, forcing the man to duck out of his master's path.

The room within was richly appointed. Brightly coloured

tapestries hung from the walls and rich rugs covered the floors. Sunlight streamed into the chamber from a window that ran the full height of the back wall, some twenty feet from the base to the ceiling. Couches and divans were arrayed around the room, alongside fine sculptures and little tables with bowls of fruit. Nearer to the wall were two chairs. Roald marched towards these and their occupants.

'It has happened at last,' he announced triumphantly. He waited for his audience to respond.

The chair to his right was occupied by a girl wearing a long white dress. Curly locks of blonde hair fell around her lace-covered shoulders. Her cherubic face brightened when she saw Roald, and she set down her knitting to devote her full attention to her father.

Seated in the other chair was a woman in her middle years. Her face was lean and aristocratic, in much the same mould as that of her husband. Baroness Hiltrude von Woernhoer was of the old blood, just as Roald was. Their families had been the first to bring civilisation to Ravensbach after the Stormcasts swept away the barbaric hordes of Chaos. The von Woernhoers were an old peerage and a proud name, so much so that Roald had surrendered his own title to adopt his wife's.

Hiltrude's current attitude was a reminder of that fact. She did not look up when Roald spoke, but just kept working at her knitting.

Roald waited. Normally he would wait as long as it took, but not today. Today he was going to demand Hiltrude's interest. 'Confound you,' he barked. 'This is important.'

'Do not be so dramatic, Roald,' the baroness countered. 'Nothing you can say could be of the slightest importance.'

Roald pounced on her dismissive words like a hungry wolf. 'Not important! Confound it, woman, put down that blasted knitting and listen!' The irritation in his tone or the persistence of his intrusion finally made Hiltrude look up. The instant she did, he thrust the message in her face. He laughed victoriously as he watched shock and wonder play through her expression.

'Is it something good, papa?' the blonde-headed girl asked.

'Better than good, Liebgarde,' Roald boasted. 'Better than your best dreams, little one.'

Hiltrude leaned back in her chair and pulled at one of her mahogany earrings. 'Can this really be?'

'You can see the count's seal right there at the bottom!' Roald stabbed his finger at the blob of wax and the impression of a castle surrounded by lightning.

'What can it mean?' Hiltrude wondered.

'Mean? Mean? Why, it means that what I've worked towards all these years is finally going to be mine.' Roald looked out of the window and watched the gardeners working in the luxurious flower beds. He despised flowers. Of all the extravagances he'd invested in, he found them the most insipid. But now he no longer resented what he'd spent on them, what he'd spent on anything. Because his name had spread throughout the great and powerful of Ravensbach. His position had grown in such stature that even Count Wulfsige had taken notice of him.

'An invitation to dinner at Mhurghast,' Roald said. 'An invitation to all of us. We are to dine with the count as his guests tomorrow.'

'But what does it mean?' Hiltrude persisted.

A cold smile crawled across Roald's patrician features. 'Count Wulfsige is old, so old it is a wonder he isn't a gheist. He has no family, no heirs to carry on his name or inherit his wealth.' His eyes gleamed as he looked at his wife and daughter. 'Don't you see? The count needs an heir. That is why he is asking us to the castle. He wants to make me his heir.'

Hiltrude was more guarded in her estimate. 'Why should he just give you what you have schemed and plotted to steal from him all these years? I know you think you are clever and hid your tracks, but maybe the count is even cleverer.'

Roald laughed at that. 'Clever? Clever? The old fool never leaves that damn castle. He's kept himself locked away in there for decades. Half of Ravensbach thinks he's already dead and it is just his servants maintaining the illusion he's alive so they don't lose their jobs. Trust me, Hiltrude, he couldn't be more oblivious if he was an ogor shopping for drapes.'

'You are always so certain of yourself, aren't you?'

'When I set my mind to something, I get it,' Roald told her. 'Though sometimes it is not quite what I thought it would be,' he added with a sneer.

'This could be one of those times,' Hiltrude warned. She directed his attention back to the invitation.

Roald read the sheet again. 'You notice it is not made out to Baroness Hiltrude von Woernhoer, but to me,' he said.

'It is not made out to Baron Roald von Woernhoer either,' Hiltrude said. This time it was her tone that had a ring of triumph to it.

Roald looked again. For an instant it escaped him, and then he finally understood what he'd glossed over in his reading of the invitation. It wasn't made out to Baron Roald von Woernhoer and family. It was addressed to Baron Roald von Rodion, his name before marrying Hiltrude.

A name he had not used in twenty years.

CHAPTER II

No one in Ravensbach was unaware of Mhurghast Castle. Built upon a high hill that overlooked the city, the ancient fortress was visible from every quarter. Its iron shadow lay across the land like a shroud, a whisper of death. Its ragged parapets stared down at the streets below with grim judgement, a merciless gaze in which all were found wanting. The central tower, its roof edged in long spikes, clawed up into the sky, blood bats and carrion crows nesting in its battlements.

When the carriage started to ascend the winding path that led to the castle, a chill of fear closed around Magda's heart. She had never been this close to Mhurghast, and now that she was all the stories from her childhood came flooding back into her mind. The children of Ravensbach often challenged one another to climb the hill and touch the castle wall. Many claimed to have done so, but they would ascend only far enough to be out of sight of their friends and duck behind one of the jagged rocks that lined the path, waiting until enough time should pass until they could return and claim to have accomplished the dare. Certainly that was what Magda had done when put to the test.

Now she was going to actually enter the site of those childhood fears. It was strange how Magda had thought herself beyond such foolishness until they were almost at their destination. She looked across the carriage to where her parents sat. Neither of them appeared uneasy in the slightest. Her mother looked excited, eager to be the guest of so wealthy a man as Count Wulfsige. Her father wasn't anxious either. He was slumped against the door, his face flushed and his eyes closed. Magda could smell the bilious liquor on his breath every time he exhaled.

Inge glanced over at Magda and rolled her eyes. 'I know,' she said. 'Your father couldn't even stay out of the bottle for one night.' She looked over at Ottokar and reached across his body to tug at the sleeve of his shirt. It had hiked up quite a bit and exposed several inches of the silver arm. As she did, her fingers struck against the hollow metal and sent a sharp sound ringing through the carriage. The noise awoke Ottokar, who spluttered and swung his bleary gaze around the carriage.

'Huh? Are we there already?'

'We're going up the hill now,' Magda said. Ottokar drew the drapery that hung over the window further back. Magda could see the steep drop on that side of the path. A matter of less than a foot and the carriage would be careening down the side to be smashed to splinters on the rocks below. A shudder swept through her, and she could feel the colour draining from her face. Ottokar was not so drunk that he didn't notice his daughter's anxiety. He quickly closed the curtain.

'It will not be long now,' Inge said, settling back in her seat. 'I rarely ask much from you, Ottokar, but this one time

I expect you to not embarrass me. Just for tonight, try to be a man and not a sot.'

Ottokar didn't respond. He just turned and stared at the closed window. It was Magda who attempted to defend him. 'Mother, you asked us to come. Father is doing his best...'

Inge sighed, long and deep. 'No. He hasn't been at his best for many years now.' She gave her husband a look that was at once both pitying and scornful. She turned back to Magda. 'Count Wulfsige invited all of us. The whole family. You don't ignore a summons like that.'

'I still don't understand why he invited us.'

'Listen,' Inge said, holding up her gloved hand. She gestured with a lace-covered finger. 'Do you hear them?'

Magda strained her ears. She could hear the rattle of their coach as it climbed the hill, but it was curiously echoed. She thought it might be some trick of the rocks throwing the sound around, until she faintly heard a horse neigh somewhere below. 'There are other coaches.'

'There are other coaches,' Inge said, her face glowing with pleasure. 'The dinner isn't just for us. Count Wulfsige is hosting a banquet.' She clapped her hands together like a little girl. 'Oh, the count used to hold the most magnificent parties. Everyone of any significance at all was there! In those days the Hauslers meant something. Your grandfather made blades fit for kings. My family, they were the richest goldmongers in the city. Oh, the feasts back then! There'd be music and dance long into the night. Sometimes it would take the first rays of dawn to put a finish to the merriment.'

'Count Wulfsige hasn't left the castle in decades,' Magda reasoned. 'Why'd he suddenly decide to host a banquet?'

'He's very old,' Inge said. 'He has no children, nothing to make him look ahead to tomorrow. So all he has are his memories of the past. Maybe he was thinking on the past and remembered the lavish parties he once held. Maybe he decided to relive those times.

'Everyone of consequence will be there,' she told Magda. 'The best families and their sons. You must be on your best behaviour. Make a good impression.' Inge frowned as she studied the understated blue dress Magda wore. 'I do wish you'd taken one of my old gowns. You need sugar to catch flies, you know.'

'I'm not interested in catching anyone,' Magda reminded her mother, hoping they weren't going to argue on the subject again. She returned Inge's gaze, evaluating her mother's low-cut gown. The shoulders were bare and the neckline plunged. The waist was drawn tight against her curves, so much so that Magda wondered how her mother was going to walk, much less dance, in the garment. 'It seems to me you've more than enough bait on display.'

Inge ignored the barb and pressed on with her attack. 'You can do better than Klueger. You should do better than him. If not for yourself, think of your children. What kind of life can a man in his profession–'

Whatever else Inge might have added to her argument went unspoken. The carriage lurched to a sudden halt. It shuddered as the coachman dropped down from his seat and walked to the door. As he opened it, Magda felt a shiver rush through her.

They were in the courtyard of Mhurghast Castle.

Iron walls surrounded them on every side, rising forty feet from the flagstones. Magda looked back at the massive gate and the steel portcullis that rose above it. Its sharpened ends seemed like fangs hanging over the gateway's gaping maw, as though at any moment it would bite down and swallow those inside the courtyard.

Magda stepped down from the carriage and turned her

eyes towards the keep. The building was as grim as the outer walls, a fortress of blackened iron. Gargoyles leered from the battlements, their mouths crusted with corrosion. The windows that peppered the imposing facade were all narrow and recessed into the edifice. The tower rose above everything, a spindle of metal ringed with savage-looking spikes near its summit. From the very peak of its roof a banner snapped in the wind, a red field with a black castle flanked by golden lightning bolts.

'Mhurghast was more cheerful back then,' Inge said as she climbed down from the carriage. She pointed to the many iron eagles that jutted from the inside walls. 'Those haven't changed though. I could never shake the impression that they were watching me.'

Following her mother's direction, Magda gave the sculptures closer scrutiny. She was surprised to find that each eagle was slightly different. Perhaps that was what accounted for their eerie, lifelike aspect. It did feel as though they were watching. More than watching – they seemed to be judging.

'They're unsettling, aren't they?'

Magda jumped. She spun around, her hand flying to her hip where her sword would be. Of course, it wasn't there. Inge might not have got her way with squeezing Magda into one of her old gowns, but she had been adamant that her daughter wasn't wearing a sword to a formal dinner.

The young man who had spoken took a step back, surprise in his eyes. 'You must be quick,' he said.

'It depends how you mean that,' Magda said coldly.

The man removed the fur cap he wore and bowed his head. 'My apologies. I didn't mean to startle you.' He smiled and nodded at the iron eagles. 'To be honest, I'm just happy to see I'm not the only one who finds those things creepy.'

Magda looked him over. He was around her own age,

handsome in a kind of rakish fashion. His clothing was respectable, if not overly opulent. Gold buttons on his vest, silver buckles on his boots. He had an ebony ring on one finger and... and she realised she was acting like her mother, evaluating people based on their appearance and how much wealth they displayed. She looked around the courtyard again. There were a few other people there, obviously guests who had arrived before the Hauslers. She saw that her mother was speaking with a man wearing the coat and hat of a Freeguild officer. He bore some resemblance to the youth who had surprised her. Magda noted with annoyance that the officer had worn his sword to the castle.

'Who says I find them creepy?' she asked, perturbed.

'I think you'd need to be one of Sigmar's chosen not to shudder with those things watching you,' the man replied. He punctuated his statement with a dramatic shiver. Such was its ridiculous excess that Magda couldn't help but laugh.

'I'm sorry,' she said, and extended her hand. 'Magda Hausler.'

The man took her hand and bowed. 'Bernger Walkenhorst.' His expression became thoughtful, and he glanced at the gloved hand he held. 'You... Forgive me for saying, but this is the wrong hand.'

Magda's cheeks turned crimson as she withdrew her left hand from him. 'I'm afraid this isn't quite... I mean, this isn't the sort...'

'It's all right,' Bernger said. His expression still showed a marked curiosity. 'This isn't my kind of thing either. I'm not really accustomed to society, as it were.'

'Then this time it's me who is relieved to not be the only one,' Magda said. She pointed to the man speaking with her mother. 'Your father? He looks like an officer.'

Bernger nodded. 'He was,' he replied. 'That was a long time ago,' he added hurriedly. His eyes still had that curious look in them. 'Forgive me if I'm impertinent, but the way you offered your hand – that's the way duellists greet people. And, well, it seemed when I startled you, you were reaching for a sword.'

Magda could see her mother looking over at them. There was an imploring sternness in her expression. 'Bad habits I've picked up,' she said. 'Not terribly ladylike, I know.'

'Of course,' Bernger said, snapping his fingers. 'Hausler. You must be the daughter of Ottokar Hausler, the swordsmith. Why, I've heard that he could not only make the finest blades, he could use them too.' The youth looked around the courtyard, obviously searching for her father.

Magda took Bernger by the arm and indicated the man he was looking for. She could actually feel the disappointment run through him, like water draining out of a waterskin. Ottokar was leaning against a short stone wall. Despite Inge's attentions, his coat was rumpled and the sleeve of his tunic had pulled back to expose part of his false arm. As though to draw further attention to his disability, Ottokar was wearing a left-handed swordbelt.

'They still tell stories about the time he was ambushed by the Karver brothers,' Bernger said. 'Just his sword against five murderers out for his blood, and it was only your father who walked away.' He turned his head and smiled at Magda. 'It's going to be an honour to break bread with a man like him.'

'Thank you for saying so.' Magda knew the words were pretence, a courtesy to salve her own disappointment. Even so, she appreciated Bernger's sympathy.

Another coach was drawing into the courtyard. Magda waited while the coachman opened the door for the occupants. A young man stepped out, his doublet and hose finer than anything either Hauslers or Walkenhorsts could afford. After him emerged an older woman with a pale complexion and deep, haunted eyes. She was followed by a man in flowing robes. The dark blue garb was edged in gold and embroidered with curious symbols and figures. The man's face had a dark, mysterious quality to it, his eyes fierce and commanding. His black hair was slicked back in a widow's peak, and when he gestured to the coachman, Magda saw that his fingers were long and sinuous, moving with an almost boneless fluidity.

'Lothar Krebs,' Bernger muttered, uneasiness in his tone. He saw the bafflement in Magda's eyes. 'The alchemist,' he added. 'I've... visited him, on occasion.'

'Perhaps my mother's right. Maybe all the people of importance have been invited to the castle.'

Bernger quickly turned away when Lothar looked in his direction. 'Shall we go inside? I'm sure the interior must be more comfortable than out here.'

Magda was rather doubtful on that score. As her eyes turned to the keep's entrance, she was struck with a sense of foreboding. The doors were standing open, huge oaken portals banded in steel, the heraldry of the von Koeterbergs branded into them. Enormous chains ran from the top of each to some mechanism buried behind the iron facade. The slabs of iron that formed the doorway were colossal, ten feet wide and half again as tall. Magda suspected they were no less imposing in their depth. How such heavy, enormous blocks of metal could have been raised to the hilltop was beyond her imagining. Legends said that Mhurghast predated the city, built by ancient wizardry long since forgotten by mortals. Gazing on it now, standing at the threshold of the keep, she could easily believe such tales.

An aged servant in a long coat embroidered with the heraldry of Count Wulfsige and fringed in fur stood just inside the entrance. The major-domo's face was pockmarked from some old affliction, his build that of a scarecrow. His smile when he bowed and greeted the guests had an oily quality to it that made Magda think of charlatans and confidence tricksters.

'Welcome, honoured guests,' the major-domo said, his unctuous voice crackling with age. 'Welcome to Mhurghast. Dinner has been prepared. If you would follow the candles, they will guide you to the dining hall. His Illustrious Highness, Count Wulfsige, will join you when the last guest has arrived.'

Bernger gave the servant a wary look. 'You didn't ask our names. How'll you know when everyone's here?'

The major-domo smiled. 'I have been instructed most carefully, mein Herr Bernger Walkenhorst. I know whom to expect, and whom to admit. If you and mein Fraulein Magda Hausler would be good enough to repair to the dining hall. Just follow the candles. If you lose your way, the other servants will set you right.'

Magda gave the major-domo a lingering look. Already Bernger had been proven wrong. Inside the castle was more unsettling than the courtyard. As they walked down the entrance hall, portraits of past von Koeterbergs glowered down at them. Golden fixtures bolted to the walls held the guiding candles, but their flickering light only magnified the illusion of animation in the pictures. She was actually relieved when she heard angry voices drifting out from one of the side corridors.

'... so sure, so certain.' The words were spoken in a female voice, the tone waspish.

'I tell you, I am the sensible heir.' A man's voice now, his words clipped and curt.

'So the count invites this motley rabble to act as an audience,' the woman said, mockery lacing her speech.

'If he does not give me what is mine by right, I'll take it from him,' the man declared. 'The old fool can't have it buried with him.'

Magda and Bernger came abreast of the corridor. They glanced into the shadowy passageway to see the arguing couple. The woman was adorned in an opulent gown, a necklace of obsidian and ebony hanging around her neck, a diamond tiara around her brow. The man's garb was equally rich, his high boots fringed in ermine and with ivory buckles running down their sides. The buttons on his silk coat were cut sapphires, contrasting with the red hue of his vestments. Several of his fingers wore rings with jewels set into the bands of wood and bone. The largest of the rings did not bear any jewels. Instead it had the crest of a snarling wolf's head with a star above it and a sword beside it.

Bernger hurried Magda along when the couple stopped their argument and glared at them. 'That was Baron and Baroness von Woernhoer,' he said. 'Next to Count Wulfsige, they might be the richest people in Ravensbach.'

'What're they doing here then?' Magda asked.

'Isn't it obvious?' Bernger said, bitterness seeping into his voice. 'The baron isn't content to be second richest. He expects to claim some sort of legacy from Count Wulfsige. His sort is never satisfied with what they have. They always have to try and grab more, no matter who they hurt.'

Magda tried to ease the outrage she heard in Bernger's words. 'Maybe the baroness is right, and he won't get a thing. That would be a fine joke on someone like him.'

Bernger smiled. 'That it would.' As they turned a corner and followed the line of candles into another hallway, his smile faltered. The grimness of the castle's dark halls closed in around them again. He gave Magda a worried look.

'I hope the joke isn't on all of us,' Bernger said. There was no humour in the way he said it, but instead a severity that sent a chill down Magda's spine.

* * *

The ivory walking stick smacked against the oak floorboards, sending strange echoes whispering through the hallways. The old man leaned heavily against it, each step seeming to drain the last of his strength. He paused and sought to draw breath into his shuddering body. It never felt like he could get enough air. Whatever prayers and potions were administered to him, he couldn't fill his lungs enough to sustain himself. It felt as though the left side of his body was always empty, the right little better. His life was ebbing away, had been for years. Only purpose had maintained him this long.

A purpose that would soon be achieved.

A servant came forwards to help him as he leaned against his stick and tried to suck air into his failing body. The old man shook the major-domo away, glowering at him from beneath his heavy brow.

'I will make my own way, Goswin,' he said. 'I have walked this path a thousand times in my dreams. Now I will do so for real.'

Goswin bowed and backed away from the old man. 'As you wish, Your Illustrious Highness.'

Count Wulfsige took another ragged breath. There was no sense in waiting. His strength would not return. All his delay did was buy his enemies a few more minutes. An ugly chuckle rattled through his wasted frame. 'I wonder if they appreciate how precious these moments are, Goswin. If they only knew.' The smile the count wore as he limped forwards once more was as grotesque as his laugh, the leer of a murderer twisting the knife in his dying victim.

'Everything is ready? They are all here?' Count Wulfsige asked his major-domo.

'There is one unaccounted for.'

'Who? Who didn't come?' Count Wulfsige swung around

with astonishing speed. His hand curled around Goswin's throat, tightening into a murderous grip.

'Notker Volkeuhn's wife,' Goswin gasped, trying to pull free from his master's strangling clutch. 'He apologised, but said she was too ill to attend.'

Count Wulfsige released him and turned away. 'The woman is of no consequence – it is her husband I want here. Notker Volkeuhn... and his child.' He stamped down the corridor, stabbing his ivory stick at the floor as though attacking an enemy.

'They are all in the dining hall, Your Illustrious Highness,' Goswin said, striding after his master. 'They have already been served.'

'And the correct dishes have been placed before those who deserve them?' Count Wulfsige demanded.

Goswin nodded. 'Everything has been carried out fastidiously. Down to the exact detail you specified.'

Count Wulfsige smiled again. 'Good. Good.' He pointed at Goswin. 'After I take my seat, you will leave. There is a coach waiting for you in the courtyard. Send the others away. The letter I have given you will allow you to see the grand lector.' He laughed again, the sound causing even his major-domo to turn pale. 'After that, there will be nothing else you need to do. The Sigmarites will attend to things.'

Master and servant continued on in silence. Count Wulfsige gazed at the ancient corridors he had known as a child, that he had grown and lived in for so many years. They were hateful to him now, as cold and deathly as a mausoleum. Yes, he had lived in this castle. He had also decayed within these walls, rotted away from the inside. He couldn't remember the happiness. All he could remember was the sorrow. The emptiness. The thirst for revenge.

Servants wearing surcoats adorned with the von Koeterberg

coat of arms opened the doors to the dining hall. Count Wulfsige stomped past them. He heard Goswin tell them to leave the doors open before the major-domo followed him into the room.

'His Illustrious Highness, Count Wulfsige von Koeterberg,' Goswin announced as his master walked towards his seat at the head of the table.

The dining hall was brightly lit, illuminated by massive chandeliers of crystal and silver. Candelabras glowed all along the walls, their light reflected by the brilliant polish of the oak floor. The table itself was a gigantic affair, stretching almost the entire length of the massive room. In the past it had seated a hundred guests, though now it was called upon to serve far fewer.

The guests were arrayed near Count Wulfsige's seat at the top of the table. Plates of carved dragonwood rested before each diner, and cedar bowls filled with spicy venison soup. The goblets that brimmed with ancient wine were cut from obsidian, the cutlery at each place setting of the finest malachite. At the centre of the table, the spread of exotic vegetables and sweetmeats was such as to impress the most cultivated connoisseur. In the midst of it all was the cooked body of a cicatrix, the less noxious cousin of the feared cockatrice. The enormous fowl had been prepared by a master chef, decorated so that it was as much a thing of spectacle as cuisine.

Count Wulfsige's glance at his guests was a cold one. A few of them sheepishly set down their spoons and knives, wondering if they should have waited for their host despite the protestations of the servants that they should begin without him.

'Eat. Eat,' Count Wulfsige encouraged them. 'If you had waited for my old carcass to hobble down here, it would all have gone cold.' He limped over to the carved seat at the head of the table. A steward drew it back for him as he sat down. He didn't look aside when he heard the doors close, but a reptilian smile spread on his visage. Goswin was leaving on his little errand.

One of the diners had stood as Count Wulfsige joined them. He raised his goblet and turned towards the head of the table. 'You have lavished us with a magnificent feast. Unparalleled by any in Ravensbach.' He turned and motioned for the other guests to stand. 'Please, join me in toasting the good health of His Illustrious Highness.'

Count Wulfsige waved everyone back into their seats. 'You do me credit, Baron von Rodion. But I fear a toast to my health would be wasting good wine. I am old, friend Roald, and near the end of my days. You should save wishes of good health for yourselves.'

Roald slowly returned to his seat. 'You are very gracious, Your Illustrious Highness.' He looked aside to his wife and then back at the count. 'Let me say that you have ever been held in the highest regard by myself and Baroness von Woernhoer. I do not think there is a finer or more noble–'

Count Wulfsige cut his speech off with a wave of his hand. 'The von Koeterbergs are an old family,' he said, his gaze roving across the table. 'We were here in the terrible days when the hordes of the Dark Gods held these lands. When the mighty Stormcasts liberated this region, it was one of my ancestors who showed them the secret path into this castle so they could overwhelm the barbarians who held it. Since that time, there has always been a von Koeterberg as master of Mhurghast.'

The old man leaned back. His eyes stalked across the table, studying each face, glancing at the plates set before them. 'When I am gone, there will be no more von Koeterbergs in Mhurghast.'

Inge Hausler spoke up, her face as beautiful as the count remembered it to be. 'Please accept my sympathy, Your Illustrious Highness.'

The smile Count Wulfsige turned on Inge was anything but friendly. 'You may keep your sympathy,' he said. 'But for you, my son Hagen would be here to continue after me.' He savoured the look of shock and horror that gripped her face. Then he pointed at the rest of the diners. 'Each of you had your part. The false friends who lied to my son. The sniffing jackals who thought to exploit him. All of you are to blame.'

The count stabbed his finger at the elderly scholar who sat near the end of the diners with his effete son beside him. 'Notker Volkeuhn, the chaplain, the pious man who would instruct my son in moral rectitude and would keep his soul from straying from that which is good and just.' As the count spoke, Notker lowered his head in shame and closed his hand around the little gold hammer that hung about his neck.

'Nushala Iliviar,' the count snarled, turning his attention to the person seated opposite Notker. She was tall and thin, her skin creamy and pale. Her features had a harsh, inhuman beauty to them, and her hair was like spun gold. Gold too was the flowing gown that graced her slender figure, the material itself alive with enchanted motion. The aelf's gaze was indifferent while she listened to Count Wulfsige speak. 'You were Hagen's tutor, the most expensive my money could buy. You know a dozen languages, are familiar with the art and science of fair Azyr. Yet what wisdom did you teach my son? What knowledge did you fill his mind with? Your son sits next to you, Nushala. Where is mine!'

Count Wulfsige pointed again, this time at the rotund finery of a short man with a long moustache seated with his wife and two children. 'Hartmann Senf, the friend and comrade-in-arms. What good was your friendship and camaraderie when my son needed it most? Did you keep him from a dark path, or did you encourage his folly?'

'I will not listen to this slander,' Roald snarled, throwing down his cutlery and rising from the table.

'You will listen,' the count hissed. 'Baron Roald von Rodion. The moneylender. The usurer. Happy to loan Hagen whatever he needed. Never concerned with what he needed it for. Never wondering why he simply wouldn't ask his father for a loan.' A crackle of bitter mirth left the old man when he saw Roald slump back in his chair. 'Ah, I see you do remember.'

The count swung around and pointed at Lothar Krebs. 'The alchemist, seeking to wrest the secrets of the realms from its constituent components. But those components cost a great deal, don't they, friend Lothar? So when you brew up something you might be able to sell, you do not scruple about who you sell it to. Hagen was only eighteen when you let him imbibe your narcotic mixture. And the more he wanted, the more it cost him. Did you even pause to consider the damage your poison was doing to him?

'Captain Bruno Walkenhorst,' the count snarled as he rounded on the former officer. 'You commanded Hagen in battle and he was proud to serve under you in the Freeguild. He looked up to you. I dare say he worshipped you. And what did you do? How did you return his loyalty and friendship? You betrayed him. You took his woman from him.'

Bruno glared at the count. 'I didn't. You can't take something away that someone doesn't have to begin with.'

'You humiliated him in a duel, sent him crawling back to Mhurghast like a whipped cur,' Count Wulfsige growled. He swung around and thrust his finger towards Inge. 'All for that wanton strumpet! Hagen loved you more than he loved himself. Oh, you were so beneath him in station, but it did not matter to Hagen. The only argument I ever had with him was when I spoke against you. For you he would defy his own father! That was the magnitude of his love! He would have cast aside his birthright for your sake.' The count's hand curled into a gnarled fist, which he shook at the shocked Inge. 'How did you return that love? You toyed with him and then cast him aside. Betrayed him with his closest friend!'

'I think you're forgettin' someone,' a gruff voice rumbled from midway down the table. A pair of bearded duardin sat between the Krebs family and Volkeuhn's. The older of the two, his beard almost pure white, glowered at the count. 'Tell me what offence you imagine I've inflicted on you. What's my connection to your son?'

For an answer, Count Wulfsige waved over one of his servants. He gave the steward his ivory walking stick and ordered him to take it to the duardin. There was visible irritation on the duardin's face as he took the object. As he turned the ivory stick over in his hands, his expression changed to one of shock.

'This has my rune on it,' he grumbled. 'How can this stick be bearin' my mark?'

'It has changed since you worked on it, Cogsmith Alrik Blackthumb,' the count explained. 'When it left your workshop, it was the frame of a very elegant, very powerful weapon.'

The count leaned forwards, his eyes glittering maliciously as he looked at his guests. 'You believe Hagen died after a long illness. Yes, he was ill. Yes, it did kill him. His mind was deluded by Lothar's concoctions and the pain of betrayal, of love rejected. So he took that thing' – he gestured to the ivory stick – 'and he put its barrel in his mouth. He had to use his toe to press the trigger, but when it was all finished the shot was true. There was so little left of his face… so very little.' The old man faltered, his viciousness draining away as a haunted look filled his eyes.

'That was twenty years ago,' Roald argued. 'You can't still be...'

The baron's words broke the melancholy that had settled upon the old man. He glowered at Roald. The smile that appeared on Count Wulfsige's face was diabolical in its malignity. 'You have never lost a child, have you, Roald? You have never felt the pain of that loss. The emptiness that gnaws at you, that makes every heartbeat hateful to you. You long for death, but there is something else you long for even more.

'Revenge.'

Alarm swept around the table. 'He's poisoned us!' came the cry. Some of the diners flung their dishes away and retreated from their seats. Others started to rush the count, but his servants had already closed in. Four men in the von Koeterberg livery surrounded their master with drawn swords.

'Sit,' the count commanded. 'No one has been poisoned. Do you think I would wait twenty years for such a simple retribution?' He sneered at the guests. 'No, poison would be far too kind.' He clenched his hand into a fist and shook it at the table. 'I will destroy you as I have been destroyed. I will destroy you through your children. You will know the crawling horror as you watch your children die. But more than die, they will come back to you, seeking your death.'

'The man is clearly insane,' Lothar pronounced.

Count Wulfsige pounced on the statement. 'Insane? Mad, am I? Mad with twenty years of hate! Mad from waiting, watching until this night. This night for my revenge.'

The old man sank back in his chair, his eyes glittering with malice. 'Have you ever heard the legend of the Mardagg? The Skullcallers know of it, and they hold it in utter dread. It is the Executioner of Khorne, the Chooser of the Damned. The barbarians worship it out of fear, marking sacrifices for it to claim so that it will spare the rest of their tribe. Never have they told an outsider how to summon the Mardagg, never have they trusted anyone with that secret.' A withering cachinnation racked the count's body. 'Until now.

'The daemon will come. The Mardagg will possess a mortal host.' Count Wulfsige pointed at the diners. 'One of your children will be its host. With that body the daemon will seek the destruction of the parents. Flesh cannot sustain such a being for long, so it will possess another host once it has used up the first.' The old man's face contorted into a mask of utter hate. 'On and on again the process will repeat. Blood will cry out for blood and the halls of this castle will echo with murder. Then my vengeance will be complete!'

'The diseased imagining of a corrupt mind,' Nushala scoffed. 'I too have heard of this daemon, but I am not so credulous to accept that a mere human could ever master an entity of such terrifying power.'

'No, not master it,' Count Wulfsige said. 'Simply give it direction to do what it would do anyway. Khorne cares not from whence the blood flows, but I do.' He swept his gaze across the table and glowered at the guests. 'Of course, a blood offering is needed to set the chain in motion.'

The count dipped his hand into his coat and drew forth a long bronze dagger. He could feel the evil that radiated from the blade. He could see from their faces that the guests could feel it too. Before anyone could react, he raked the phurba across his own throat.

Count Wulfsige slumped forwards onto the table, blood gushing from his slashed throat, steaming as it spattered across the table. The pool of gore bubbled and boiled. Soon the blood became a dark and pungent smoke that wafted up towards the chandeliers, but evaporated before reaching the lights.

The armed servants dropped their swords and backed away

from their dying master. Count Wulfsige lifted his head and stared one last time at his enemies. A malevolent grin froze on his face as he dropped back onto the table.

Far off, from the temples down below in Ravensbach, bells began to ring. They were noting the setting of the sun and the advent of night, but to those inside Mhurghast they seemed to be a dirge for Count Wulfsige and the von Koeterbergs.

A dirge for the man who had damned them all with his final breath.

CHAPTER III

Magda put her hand to her mouth to stifle her cry as she watched Count Wulfsige's horrific demise.

'The man was mad,' Roald pronounced, breaking the momentary spell of silence. 'His claims were mad, his schemes were mad.' He wagged his finger at the corpse. 'There is all the proof you need. A madman with more wealth in his coffers than wits in his head.'

Hartmann dabbed his napkin across his sweaty brow. 'Yes… yes. The count was mad,' the merchant hurriedly agreed. 'His claims… completely outrageous.'

Magda turned to her parents. Inge had a strange look in her eyes, an expression she had never seen there before. Was it regret, or guilt? Surely it wasn't shame? Beside her, Ottokar was tapping his finger against his obsidian goblet. His face had a sickly pallor, but his eyes weren't bleary from wine. They were clear and focused… and hurt. He didn't raise his glass. It seemed he had no taste for wine right now.

'Call the count mad if it makes you feel better,' Nushala said, her fine aelfen voice wafting across the table like doleful music. 'But he was not so mad as to not know what he was speaking of. From his perspective I failed to instruct his offspring correctly. I am not so ignorant of humans that I cannot see that each of you agrees with what he said about you.' She raised her slender hand as Roald clenched his fist. 'Whatever your protestations, each of you feels guilty inside for what the count laid at your feet.'

Alrik's son, Brond, kicked his chair away and glowered at the aelf. 'And what about you, tall-ears?' the duardin growled. 'You admit you failed the count's whelp?'

Nushala simply shrugged, the living gold of her gown rippling with the motion. 'A human mind can little appreciate the nuances of instruction. They operate upon such a shallow level.' She brushed aside her son's hand when he tried to keep her from continuing. 'It must be said that humans simply cannot understand anything that rejects their preconceptions. That the labour of a few decades or even a few centuries is of no consequence. Of course I feel I failed to educate the boy – how could it have been otherwise? He could barely appreciate the surface of knowledge, much less plunge into the deeps of true wisdom.'

'Arrogant, insufferable, miserable aelves,' Bernger said suddenly. 'You sneer down your nose at the work of men! What great things has your kind ever accomplished? Slinking about with puffed-up airs while enjoying the protection of whoever you can exploit! You're half witch and half daemon – it's no wonder you would laugh at a dying man's curse!'

'It would be unwise for any of us to laugh at Count Wulfsige's curse,' Notker said. The former priest clenched the gold hammer he wore so tightly that his knuckles turned white. 'The Mar–the daemon he named is real. It is named in the *Liber Daemonium* as one of the profane Blood God's most monstrous visitations. A remorseless spectre, an elemental force of death. Not the clean death that must come to all mortals, but the unholy slaughter that rends the soul. It is not the underworlds of Nagash to which the spirits of its victims descend, but rather the endless torment of the Blood God's obscene domain.'

Lothar rose from his seat and made a placating motion with his hands. 'I fear you antagonise these good people to no purpose, Volkeuhn. Your knowledge of the names and character of daemons may be extensive' – the alchemist smiled – 'but I fear you are forgetting that in magic – even the blackest magic – there are always rules. Rituals that must be followed exactly in order for the sorcery to manifest. Count Wulfsige spoke–'

'What does any of this matter?' Inge cried out. She pointed to the corpse at the head of the table. 'How can you all keep talking with *that* lying right beside you?'

Magda had seen her mother's agitation swelling, her eyes darting back to the count's body, her lips trembling with horror.

Bruno spoke up in agreement. 'The lady's right. Perhaps we should talk this through, but it's obscene to do so while our late host is in our company.'

'You there,' Roald called out to the valets. 'See to your master.' When they hesitated, the baron fixed them with his most imperious glare. 'Do as I say.'

'You had better do as my husband requests,' Hiltrude warned them. 'At least, if you hope to find another position somewhere in Ravensbach.'

The threat overcame the servants' trepidation, and the men took hold of the dead count. Magda watched in morbid fascination as they gathered up the corpse, taking pains to wrap the head in a napkin as if in fear that it might fall off. One of the valets paused beside the hideous knife. He snatched the napkin from in front of Ottokar and used it to recover the weapon. The men soon withdrew with their gruesome burden.

Nushala motioned to Lothar. 'Before you were interrupted you had been saying something about how magic works. I should be very interested to be educated on the subject.'

Lothar gave the aelf a dark look. 'I was simply reminding everyone of what the count claimed would happen. That the daemon he would conjure would infest our children – one by one – and that through them it would seek to murder us.' He paused as several of his companions gasped. 'A horrible thing to claim, but I assure you well beyond the man's ability to make reality.'

The alchemist stopped and turned to Notker again. 'Mind you, I am only speaking from theory rather than practice. I should hardly enjoy leaving here to find the Order of Azyr waiting at my home.'

'Forget about witch hunters and get to the point,' Roald snapped. Magda wasn't taken in by the baron's veneer of superiority and position. He seemed to be on the verge of losing all restraint and running from the room.

'The *point*, Baron von Woernhoer, is that there are certain occult rituals that must be observed to make a physical host ready for a daemon.' Lothar raised his glass. 'Before you can pour the wine there must be a suitable vessel to receive it. There would also need to be an incantation to summon it.'

Magda's eyes went wide at Lothar's words. Something that had struck her as strange earlier now came back to her with monstrous implications. 'When we were seated,' she said. She looked at her parents. 'Remember, when the steward showed us to our places?'

Inge's voice was sharp with tension. 'He simply said our names and indicated the chairs we were to take.'

'No, that isn't right,' Bernger said. He looked to his father for confirmation. 'When he showed you to your seat he said, "This is your chair." But when myself and Magda were shown in, what he said was, "Bernger Walkenhorst, accept the place prepared for you." Those were his exact words.'

Magda nodded. 'That's what he said to me. "Magda Hausler, accept the place prepared for you." But he did not use those words when my parents were seated.'

Other affirmations came from around the table as the children of Count Wulfsige's guests recalled the manner in which they had been seated. Roald turned and fixed the servants with a demanding look. 'Where is that steward? I want him to account for this!'

The servants looked among themselves. Finally one of the maids stepped forwards. 'Please, your lordship, but Herr Goswin isn't here.'

'Well, find the cur!' Roald snarled. 'I want him to explain this foolishness.' He glared at the servants until they hurried off to find the absent major-domo.

Lothar gave Magda a patient smile. 'You think such an innocent phrase can conjure a daemon?' There was a cynical mockery in his tone that caused her to scowl back at him. In the best circumstances she had no tolerance for that kind of patronising smugness.

'I should not be so quick to dismiss the possibility, alchemist,' Nushala said, her tone as haughty as Lothar's. 'The ritual might have been performed before we arrived. Left incomplete. Waiting for the final... I am not sure there is an adequate concept in your philosophy, so let us say *consecration*. With those mundane words spoken by Goswin, whatever curse Count Wulfsige plotted may have been brought to fruition.'

Notker banged his fist against the table. 'No!' he shouted. 'It cannot be. Mighty Sigmar has confounded the Ruinous Powers. They cannot manifest except in flesh that has been marked for the Dark Gods.' He shook off his son's hand as he slammed his fist again and again on the table. 'None here could be so abominable as to have the mark of Chaos upon them.'

Notker was in what amounted to a fit now. One hand clenched the hammer icon so tightly that blood dripped from his fist. The other continued to pound the table. Plates and bowls were jostled by the vibrations. Those in front of his son, Reiner, were upended and spilled to the floor. Hartmann's daughter reached down to recover the fallen objects. Herlinde set the bowl on the table, but as she picked up the plate the girl screamed and threw it across the room. Shrieking, she cowered against her mother, unable to speak for the frightened sobs racking her.

Brond moved from his chair and walked over to the plate. He picked it up, and as he did his expression became dour. He hurried back to the table and seized the plate he had been supping from. Tossing the remaining food on the floor, he turned it over and stared at the underside.

'What is it?' Alrik asked. Magda wasn't certain, but she thought she could see anxiety in the duardin's eyes.

The younger duardin didn't answer. He simply turned both plates over and showed their undersides to the rest of the guests. Drawn upon the bottom of both plates was a grisly sigil.

'Sigmar preserve us!' Sigune Senf cried, and held her daughter close.

'The Skull Rune of Khorne,' Nushala gasped, her shock such that the aelf forgot her lofty arrogance.

'The mark is not upon the flesh,' Lothar proclaimed. 'It has been taken into the flesh! Whatever was set upon the plates was consecrated to the Blood God, and by eating it, by consuming the food, the mark was drawn into...' He swung around and turned over his own plate. A sigh of relief rose from the alchemist when he found that there was no mark.

All around the table, others were upending their settings, checking their plates, bowls, cups, even cutlery for the gruesome symbol. It soon became clear that only the plates had been touched. And only certain plates.

Magda sat shivering as she gazed upon the grotesque rune drawn upon hers in blood. She looked across the table and saw Bernger gazing at his own plate in a kind of numb horror.

'All of the children,' Hartmann stated. 'He marked only the children's plates, and the steward only recited those words when he seated the children.'

Nushala turned to her son. 'Did you eat anything?' Abarahm dipped his head in reluctant acknowledgement.

The question, however, provoked an immediate reaction from Roald. Lunging from his chair, he seized his daughter by the shoulders. 'You didn't eat anything,' he said. 'Tell me you didn't eat anything, Liebgarde!'

Hiltrude stood up and cracked her hand across Roald's face. He rubbed at his cheek while she knelt beside their daughter. 'It is no good pretending. All of us are at the same risk. All of our children ate from their own plates.'

'The daemon will come,' Notker groaned. There were tears in his eyes as he looked at Reiner. 'It will do what Count Wulfsige called it to do. It will kill all of us through our own children!'

Magda was surprised when her father suddenly stood up. Ottokar gave her a sad, wistful smile, then turned and spoke to the others at the table. 'May I ask one thing? If we accept that there's some murdering daemon coming to possess our children, then why by all the underworlds are we just sitting around waiting for it?'

Lothar seized on the idea. 'To call a powerful daemon requires everything to be exact. That includes the place in which it is expected to manifest.'

'Mhurghast was once used by the barbarians as a citadel,' Bruno said. 'Even now it has a sinister quality to it. Surely all of you have felt it.'

'A residual taint,' Nushala said. 'A trace of Chaos that has seeped into the very walls. The least echo, biding its time to be awakened again.' The aelf shook her head. 'Yes, such a place would ease the passage of a daemon.'

'Then if we are in agreement on that question,' Hiltrude said, 'let's stop wasting time and get out of here!'

Of everyone who had spoken, Magda thought the baroness made the most sense.

Bernger was close behind his father as they left the dining hall. Hiltrude's suggestion had been taken with nary a protest. Indeed, the only voices that had been raised in objection had been those of the duardin and Bruno Walkenhorst. Bernger had little experience with the Ironweld, as it was generally considered a bad idea to steal from the stocky duardin. As famous as they were for the quality and craftsmanship of their wares, they were equally infamous for the excessive vindictive streak that seemed ingrained in every one of them. Slight a duardin and they would bear that grudge against your grandchildren's grandchildren. Alrik and his son wanting to stay and somehow make a stand struck Bernger as sheer obstinacy more than anything else.

Why Bruno wanted to remain was more of a puzzle. But then Bernger had learned things tonight that he had never known about his father. It was clear that Count Wulfsige's accusations about Bruno and Inge were closer to the mark than not. He wanted to ask him about his version of what had happened, whether he had truly betrayed Hagen or if that part of it was merely the count's bitter interpretation. It would be an impolitic subject to broach, but Bernger needed to know. He needed to understand the specifics of whatever had happened between Bruno and Magda's mother.

'Thunder and hammer!' Roald cursed as he led the group away from the dining hall. 'Where are those damn servants?'

'Looking for Goswin, your lordship,' Lothar reminded him. 'Don't you remember sending them all away?'

Roald turned his scowl from the five corridors that led up to the dining hall and fixed the angry look at Lothar's sardonic face. 'One of the swine could have had sense enough to stay behind.'

Bernger frowned at the nest of hallways. 'Does anyone remember which corridor we came down?'

'This one,' Roald declared, and started for the centremost hallway. Like the others, it was dimly illuminated by a few sputtering candles. There was no trace of the bright displays that had served to guide them before.

The two aelves headed for the inner-left passage, their raiment of living gold writhing about their tall, lean frames. 'It is this one,' Nushala said.

Hartmann barked with scornful laughter. 'We're just going to follow an aelf on her say-so? They're probably in league with the daemon. Leading us to it so they can bargain with it and save their own lives.'

Several of the others took up the merchant's track, casting their own aspersions on the trustworthiness of aelves. Magda wasn't one of them. 'You've nothing to justify such claims, Herr Senf,' she said. 'Only rumour and superstition.'

'The lass is right,' grumbled Alrik, his face looking as

though he'd swallowed something repugnant. 'You can call an aelf a flouncy fop without the mettle for honest work, but you can't question that snare-trap memory they have. If an aelf tells you it was rainin' at a specific hour four years ago, then you can bet it was rainin'. If she says this is the way, this is the way.'

Nushala gave the entire group an indifferent stare. 'Follow me or don't. If you want to get lost in here, it is no difference to me.' With her son following in her wake, she started off down the left hallway.

'Well, that convinces me,' Ottokar declared. He took hold of Magda's hand and led her after the aelves. Inge was close behind them, asking the swordsmith if he was sure but receiving no answer.

Bernger looked at his father. 'Let's follow them,' he said. 'If anything's wrong, they'll need help.'

Bruno gave Bernger a wry look, but finally nodded. His hand fell to the sabre he wore, another relic from his days as a Freeguild captain. 'I've heard it said it takes a blade of cold iron to hurt an aelf. If those two are up to anything, we'll put that to the test.'

Bernger and his father set off, joined by the duardin. Soon the rest of the guests were following down the hall. Bernger could hear Roald complaining that they were going the wrong way, but the baron's objections weren't enough to keep him from following them.

Bernger quickened his step and hurried to join the Hauslers. Inge gave a start when he caught up to them, her mind clearly on other things. Ottokar nodded by way of greeting. Bernger felt a warmth flash through him when Magda turned and smiled at him. 'Father and I were concerned. If Nushala is planning any–'

'They say an aelf can hear an ant crawling up a leaf from

a mile away,' Ottokar said. 'You may want to be a bit more guarded with whatever you wanted to say.'

Embarrassment coloured Bernger's cheeks. 'I just wanted to say, whatever happens, my father and I will help.' He glanced at the sword hanging from Ottokar's right hip. 'I can use a blade.'

'So can my father,' Magda said, anger tingeing her words. 'For that matter, so can I.'

'A graceless conceit for a young lady,' Inge said. Her anxious gaze swept the stark iron walls around them and the grim portraits of old von Koeterbergs glaring down at them. 'Though right now I begin to think...' She smiled awkwardly at Magda and then quickly looked to Ottokar. 'Don't be foolish. Give your sword to this young man. He has two good arms to use it.'

Bernger did not think he'd ever seen someone's expression descend into complete fury as quickly as Magda's did when she heard Inge's words. Such was her rage that she couldn't speak, only stare in mute abhorrence.

Ottokar simply shrugged, a peculiar motion since it failed to so much as shake his right arm. 'I'll trust no hand but my own to guard my daughter,' he said. His eyes strayed over to Bernger. 'I thank you and Bruno for all the help you care to give, but while I can still draw and slash, I'm keeping my sword.'

Bernger was struck by the intensity of the swordsmith's voice. The sot who had staggered around in the courtyard was gone, only some faint echoes of his presence lingering on in the corners of Ottokar's eyes. 'I'll support you in whatever way I can.'

'Don't be stubborn!' Inge argued. 'You aren't the brash duellist any more. The boy can do more with that sword than you can.'

The anger that had been boiling inside Magda burst forth. 'Maybe, mother, if you had a loyal thought in that strumpet brain you would appreciate father! Hagen, Bruno – how many other men have you enjoyed? That cogsmith didn't bring a wife with him!'

'Don't speak to your mother that way,' Ottokar snapped. He waved his hand at the next turn in the hall, where a flash of gold was just disappearing around the corner. 'If we keep bickering, we'll lose sight of the aelves.'

The little group continued on in silence. Bernger could feel the anger rolling off Magda and Inge. The daughter kept directing black looks at her mother. The few glances she turned his way were little better. Resentment over whatever past association Bruno had with Inge, he decided. He wondered how long that relationship had gone on. Was it after her marriage to Ottokar?

Bernger looked back and waved to his father. He gestured to indicate the corner they were turning. Bruno acknowledged the direction and said something to the duardin. Farther back, the rest of the guests advanced in a bunched crowd. Bernger strained, but he couldn't hear Roald grousing over his injured pride. Perhaps the baroness had finally told him to shut up.

Turning the corner, Bernger was surprised to find that Ottokar had drifted back, waiting for him. There was a grave look in his eyes as he regarded him. 'If anything happens, promise me you'll get them out,' he whispered, jerking his chin at Magda and Inge. The two women were about ten feet ahead of them, hurriedly pursuing the aelves.

'I will,' Bernger said, the words coming before he really gave thought to what they might entail. 'I'll get them out.'

Ottokar slowly followed his family. 'Promise me you'll keep Magda from... If I can't go with her, you have to make her accept that.' A strange, sad smile appeared on his face. 'She's always been headstrong. Takes after me in all the wrong ways.'

'I'll get her out,' Bernger assured him. His eyes drifted to the swordsmith's silver arm. A horrible thought came to him. It was spoken before he could restrain himself. 'Your arm. Did you lose it in a duel with my father?'

Ottokar slapped his false arm, the hollow ring of the silver shell echoing down the hall. Magda and Inge looked back, worry in their gaze. 'This? This was much later. And it wasn't your father who was responsible. Bruno Walkenhorst was a fearsome swordsman, but if we'd ever crossed blades you might not be here today. No, this wound came from someone else. Someone who didn't scruple about cheating.' He gave Bernger a reassuring pat on the shoulder. 'Bruno was never the sort of man who could beat me, and he wouldn't cheat in a fight. The man who did this did it for money. He's dead now, and the man who hired him lost interest soon after.'

'What was at issue?' Bernger asked.

'I've told you what I've told you to allay worries about your father's integrity,' Ottokar said. 'The rest doesn't concern you.' He strode forwards to join the women. 'Hang back a bit so the others don't get lost, but see that you keep us in sight as well.'

They turned down two more side passages before again reaching the main hallway. Bernger could see the aelves ahead of them. Nushala was speaking with a group of twenty or so servants who were clustered in the middle of the hall. Beyond them, just visible at the end of the corridor, was a bright glow. For a moment he was confused. It should be early evening. There couldn't be any sunlight in the courtyard. Then his ears caught the faintest trace of sound. It was the low murmur of many voices.

Abarahm turned when Bernger and the Hauslers approached.

It was difficult to read the aelf's face, but it seemed to him there was a certain grimness in his visage. 'The count's servants tried to leave the castle. They were stopped.'

'You stopped them?' Magda asked.

The aelf took a moment to answer her. 'No. My mother and I came afterwards.' He gestured to where Nushala crouched over the prostrate figure of a coachman. The man's cream-coloured vest was stained crimson by the oozing wound in the middle of his chest.

'Bullet,' Ottokar said. 'Who shot him?'

One of the maids shook a trembling hand at the end of the corridor. 'They did. The men from Ravensbach.'

'They said no one could leave the castle,' elaborated a cook. 'They said they'd kill anyone who tried.'

'They won't keep us here,' Ottokar snarled. His left hand curled around the grip of his sword. Inge grabbed him, pinning his arm between their bodies.

'Don't be a fool!' she cried. 'Wasn't it enough to be shot once?'

The remark brought a flash of pain to Ottokar's expression, but also dulled the reckless heroism of a moment before. He pressed his lips to Inge's. 'If I thought I could buy you time to get away, I'd do it gladly,' he said.

'We wouldn't leave you,' Magda insisted. She gave Inge an imploring look. 'Tell him we wouldn't leave him.' When her mother remained silent, she pushed her away and gripped her father's arm. 'We wouldn't leave you,' she vowed.

Ottokar raised his hand to his daughter's head, running his fingers through her hair.

Bernger looked back at the coachman. 'Can you do anything for him?' he asked Nushala.

The aelf gave him a curious look. A chill rippled through Bernger. Until he'd said something, had it not occurred to her to try and aid the man? Nushala's long fingers pulled back the bloodied garment and exposed the ugly wound.

'You'd be wastin' your time,' Alrik grumbled gruffly. The cogsmith had reached the cluster of servants and was now standing over the coachman. 'I know you tall-ears have enough time to waste it, but some of us don't.' The duardin pointed at the bits of tissue that peppered the man's vest. 'Bullet smacked right through a lung. He must've been hit from up-close.'

'Otto was shot by one of the Freeguild,' a valet stated. 'Couldn't have been more than six paces between them when he fired.'

'Freeguild?' Bruno asked as he joined them. The other duardin stepped in to join Alrik.

'The castle's been sealed off,' Bernger reported, waving at the servants. 'Men from Ravensbach are in the courtyard and have threatened to kill anyone who tries to leave.'

'Audacious,' Nushala proclaimed as she rose to her feet. 'I should like to see them try.' She turned, looking as though she might march straight to the courtyard. Abarahm laid his hand on her shoulder, holding her back while the two conversed in their lilting language.

Inge walked over to the aelves. 'It might be best to wait for Baron von Woernhoer. He's a man of importance in Ravensbach. Surely these men in the courtyard will listen to his authority.'

Nushala turned a withering look on Inge, but there was gratitude in Abarahm's eyes. 'Let the stupid little man have his moment of importance,' Nushala said.

'What about the coachman?' Bernger asked. 'Maybe the alchemist could...'

Alrik shook his head. 'Lad, unless Lothar is also a necromancer, there's nothin' he can do now. The man's dead.'

Some of the maids began to cry as the cogsmith made his

pronouncement. A butler stepped forwards to drape his coat over the corpse.

The remainder of the dinner guests came marching towards the macabre scene. 'What happened to him?' Hartmann asked, his voice becoming shrill as he noted the blood on the floor beside the body.

'Damnation take the wretch!' Roald exclaimed. The baron glared at the surviving peasants. 'Where is Goswin? Have you found the scoundrel?'

Magda stalked over to Roald. 'We have bigger problems, your lordship,' she said, twisting the address so it sounded almost profane. 'Soldiers, men from Ravensbach, have assembled in the courtyard. They aren't letting anyone leave the castle.' She pointed at the dead coachman. 'They'll kill anyone who tries.'

'Oh they will, will they?' Roald sneered, his face contorted with contempt. 'We will just see about that.' He stormed down the hallway towards the brightly lit courtyard. The other guests and some of the servants followed after him.

'It's just possible the pompous nob will make them back down,' Bernger said to Magda.

She looked over at Hiltrude and Liebgarde. 'Maybe he'll get his family out,' Magda said. 'But he couldn't care less about what happens to the rest of us.'

There was too much truth in Magda's observation for Bernger to argue with her. The flicker of hope that had been there only a moment before evaporated.

As the procession neared the end of the corridor, a harsh voice shouted above the general murmur. 'You there! That is far enough! No one's leaving Mhurghast!'

Roald stiffened at the challenge. 'You dare address me in that tone, dog! I am Baron Roald von Woernhoer!' His head back, his shoulders set, he brazenly marched towards the entrance.

Bernger braced himself for the crack of a gun. Instead there was the sharp hiss of a bow loosing an arrow.

Roald cried out as a feathered shaft struck his hand, piercing it just behind his thumb. The arrowhead emerged from his palm, blood spraying from the wound. The baron staggered back and waved his other hand in submission. 'I'm going back! I'm going back!' he cried.

'So much for the privileges of rank,' Lothar remarked as the injured Roald retreated towards them.

'Fanatics!' Roald cursed. He held his injured hand so Hiltrude could see it. 'When we leave here I will have every one of them strung up by their thumbs and fed to the carrion crows!'

Hiltrude gave the injury a brief glance. 'Is there someone who could do something about this? I don't want my husband dripping all over my dress.'

'The aelf tried to help Otto,' one of the valets suggested, clearly remembering things differently than Bernger did.

Mention of Nushala had Bernger looking around for her. He cried out in alarm when he finally saw her. While everyone else was looking at Roald, she had started down the corridor towards the courtyard. His cry made no difference to Nushala, but it did draw her son's notice.

'Mother!' Abarahm shouted. 'Come back! They will shoot you!'

Nushala kept advancing, her gown of living gold rippling about her slender body. 'Preposterous,' she said. 'They would not dare.'

Bernger grabbed hold of Abarahm before he could race after his mother. He swung around and tried to wrench free of Bernger's grip. There was a steely strength in the aelf's slim arm that surprised Bernger. He surprised the aelf when his fist smacked Abarahm's chin and dropped him senseless to the floor.

'By Grungni's Beard,' Alrik growled. 'Tall-ears is goin' to pull it off.'

Bernger and the others watched as Nushala marched past the spot where Roald had been shot. As she advanced, the dazzling glow of torches retreated ahead of her. He could now see something of the nature of the men in the courtyard. The uniforms of Freeguild soldiers, the habits of Sigmarite monks, the coarse tunics of labourers and the colourful doublets of burghers. All of the men gave ground before the stern aelf, their faces drawn with superstitious dread. Pistols and crossbows were lowered as the mob backed away.

Then, from behind the mob a strident voice called out, 'Hold your ground! Do not retreat before evil!' The speaker pushed his way to the fore of the crowd. He was arrayed in white robes edged in gold, and upon his head was a silver mitre with a badge displaying the twin-tailed comet. In one hand he held a massive warhammer, in the other a ponderous tome. He raised both into the air as he addressed the faltering mob.

'Are your convictions so feeble that you balk at what must be done!' the warrior priest shouted. 'Do you fear an aelf's curse more than the threat that now hangs over all of Ravensbach? Would you let the daemon slip free to slaughter your families in their beds?' He swung the hammer around and pointed it at the castle. 'Withdraw into Mhurghast. The taint of evil is upon the place, and we will allow none touched by it to leave!'

Nushala stopped just outside the entry. 'The evil conjurations of madmen are of no concern to aelves, Grand Lector Sieghard. There is no taint of sorcery upon either myself or my son.' She took another step towards the crowd. 'Each of us has dwelt in your holy city of Azyrheim. Are you so audacious as to suggest any corruption could strike us low?'

The words made an impact on the crowd. Uncertainty rippled through them. Only Sieghard was unfazed. The warrior priest stood his ground.

'If what you say is true, withdraw into the castle,' Sieghard declared. 'No harm can befall you there if you are immune to the kiss of Chaos and the claws of the daemon. The acolytes of the temple are scouring the records for a rite of exorcism that can break this foul enchantment. Abide within the castle until we can be certain–'

Nushala glared at Sieghard. 'Impertinence,' she snapped. 'You would dare try to restrain me?' She started towards the warrior priest and a shot suddenly rang out. The aelf stumbled back as a bullet slammed into her chest. Then a second bullet struck her. And a third. By the time her body wilted to the ground, she had been hit five times. As life ebbed from her, a soldier with a pike came forwards and rolled her back into the castle.

'No one will leave Mhurghast,' Sieghard vowed. 'We have been warned! We have been told of the abominable horror that walks within those halls! It will not break free. It will not threaten Ravensbach.'

Bernger looked at Magda. 'Warned? Who could've warned them?'

A moment later Bernger had his answer. Two monks emerged from the crowd, each holding the end of a rope. They were connected to a collar locked around the neck of a third man. Bernger recognised him as the count's major-domo. The monks drew close to the entrance and jerked the ropes. Goswin was sent stumbling forwards. As he moved past them, the monks released their ropes and let the man fall prone across Nushala's body.

'All who have been exposed to this evil must be cleansed,' Sieghard pronounced. 'Not a trace of this corruption can be allowed to escape.'

Goswin scrambled away from the entrance and fled down the corridor while shots rang out behind him. As he reached the guests, Bruno caught hold of the errant major-domo.

'So that's what happened to you,' Bruno snarled. 'Went slinking off to tell Grand Lector Sieghard what your master was plotting?'

'No, I only tried to get away,' Goswin protested. He clutched at his shoulder, where one of the bullets had struck him.

Roald fixed the major-domo with a murderous stare. 'I'll get the truth out of you if I have to peel every inch of skin from your hide. You'll tell us all about the count's plot against us!'

Thilo Krebs and Reiner helped Bruno drag Goswin away. Roald nodded to Lothar. 'You're the nearest thing to a healer we have. Come along and see that the cur doesn't die before I find out what I want to know.'

As the guests and servants began to file back down the corridor, Bernger looked for someone to help him carry the stunned Abarahm. It was then that he noticed Magda creeping towards the courtyard. He hurried after her.

'What're you doing?' Bernger demanded.

Magda twisted from his grip. She didn't try to move any closer, but she did shout to the men in the courtyard. 'Please! Someone! Someone who can hear me! Find Klueger. Tell him that Magda Hausler is in here. Magda Hausler! Klueger!'

The only answer to her shouts was the indistinct murmur of the crowd. Bernger coaxed her back down the corridor. 'They won't listen,' he said. 'They won't help. If Sieghard can figure out a way, they'd rather burn down Mhurghast and everyone in it.'

'Klueger can help,' Magda said, her voice low, as though she were afraid to hear the desperation bound to her words. 'If only they would get word to him, Klueger could help.'

Bernger eased Magda back down the hallway. She helped

him pick up Abarahm when they reached the unconscious aelf. 'Who is Klueger?' he asked as they started after the others. 'How can he help?'

Magda only answered the first question. Perhaps even she was afraid to answer the second.

'Klueger is a member of the Order of Azyr,' she said. 'A witch hunter.'

CHAPTER IV

Roald decided that the parlour just off the main hallway was suitable enough for the affair at hand. He recalled it from previous visits to Mhurghast. The room was spacious, pleasantly appointed with expensive oak panels on the walls and thick rugs on the floors. More importantly, it had a hearth.

The baron had need of that hearth right now.

The guests filed into the parlour, bearing Goswin along with them. Roald pointed to one of the heavy chairs, and the major-domo was forced down into the seat. Then he motioned to Bruno and indicated that he should start a fire.

'You will save us all a lot of time and unpleasantness if you just tell us what we want to know,' Roald said as he paced between Goswin and the hearth. 'Right now you perhaps think you won't say anything, but I assure you that you will.'

Notker shook his head, a look of anguish on his face. 'Surely there is another way,' he pleaded.

'Don't fret over this rat,' Hartmann snarled, pointing to the major-domo. 'Any moment, that *thing* could possess one of our children! Burn him down to the bone, but make him talk!'

Sigune stifled a scream and drew her children close to her. 'Sigmar preserve us!'

For the first time, Goswin seemed to appreciate the grisly import of the fire Bruno was stoking. Colour fled from his visage and sweat began to bead across his brow. He glanced around, his eyes imploring the others in the room. Even the servants who had followed them into the parlour displayed little sympathy for the major-domo.

'If he can tell us anything about Count Wulfsige's plot, then we need to hear it,' Inge stated. 'It's not a question of only our survival, but that of our children as well,' she added, looking over at Magda.

'It is my family that moves me to be ruthless,' Roald explained, gesturing to Hiltrude and Liebgarde. 'For myself, I might take a risk, but I will take no chances with those most dear to me.' From the corner of his eye he watched his wife and daughter. Of course, Liebgarde was impressed with his show of concern, the spoiled idiot, but there was no change in emotion from the baroness.

'Can we trust anything revealed by torture?' Bernger asked. Abarahm was sprawled across a divan, and the youth was standing over the aelf as though seeking to do penance for knocking him senseless.

'The witch hunters trust it enough,' Lothar pointed out. Then a cynical smile appeared. 'Of course, a man will say most anything if he thinks it will stop the pain.'

Goswin swung around and nodded emphatically at the alchemist. 'I'll tell you whatever you want to know! There's no need to do... anything.'

Roald picked an iron poker from the rack beside the hearth and thrust it into the flames. 'Make me believe you,' he said.

'Convince me that I won't need to put this against your hide.' He tapped the end of the poker with his finger, his eyes fixed upon Goswin's.

Hiltrude opened the interrogation. 'Those men in the courtyard – you brought them?'

Goswin nodded. 'I was carrying out the count's command. He said I was to inform the Sigmarite priests that a daemon had been set loose in Mhurghast, that it was trying to find a body to act as its host.' He looked across the guests, searching for anyone who would show him sympathy. 'I was to tell them that the daemon would go amok in the streets of Ravensbach if it escaped the castle.'

'But that's not why Count Wulfsige conjured it,' Magda interrupted. 'He claimed it was called up for revenge. Revenge against all of us.'

Roald stormed over to Goswin's chair, towering over the man. 'Well, how do you explain that? Were you privy to what the count was planning?'

'I only know what I was told to tell the priests,' Goswin said. 'I don't know what else–'

'That'd be a lie,' Alrik snorted. He jabbed his thumb at the major-domo. 'It was you who spouted that rigmarole when you were showin' everybody where to sit.' He nodded at Lothar. 'That smacked of wizardry, accordin' to those who know a bit about such things.'

'Make him talk before the daemon comes,' Hartmann demanded, his eyes darting to his children. 'Have him tell us how to stop it!'

Roald ignored the merchant and leaned close to Goswin. 'Lies?' he hissed venomously into his ear. 'Do you really think you are in a position to deceive me? The question of how much I have to hurt you really depends on how much I believe you. But perhaps you would rather start over?'

'Yes! Yes, I admit it. Count Wulfsige told me exactly what to say when I brought each of you to the table.' Goswin's voice rose to a ragged squeal. 'I didn't know there was importance... I didn't know what he was planning...'

Notker walked to the major-domo, his son following close behind him. The former priest glared at Goswin. 'You had to know,' he said. 'You have served the count long enough to know the significance of that hellish rune on those plates!'

Goswin cringed back in the chair, but only for a moment. A crafty look crept into his eyes. 'Perhaps I do know what you're saying,' he said. He looked around at the other guests and then back to Notker. 'Would you like me to tell everyone how? As you say, I have been in Mhurghast a very long time.'

Roald drove his fist into Goswin's face and knocked the major-domo back. 'Damn your plotting, you cur!' The baron wiped his bruised knuckles on the fabric of the chair. 'You'll talk to me! You'll tell me what I want to know!'

'Make him talk fast,' Hartmann whined.

Roald glanced over at the frantic merchant, then at the rest of the guests. The last thing any of them needed was Hartmann's reminders about the doom hanging over them. 'Talk,' he demanded, raising his fist to strike Goswin again.

'Yes, your lordship,' Goswin said as he wiped blood from his bruised mouth. He gestured at Notker. 'The count... He brought Volkeuhn back after he'd been discharged from Mhurghast fifteen years ago. I escorted him around the castle. I led him... No, he led me, to places that had been–'

Notker started to grab at Goswin. Roald intervened and held the former priest back. Despite his age, Notker was intent on getting hold of the major-domo. 'Help me,' Roald snapped at the other guests. 'The old fool has gone mad!' Bruno and Bernger hurried to aid the baron. Each took hold of an arm and dragged the cleric back. Reiner lunged at the two men who had seized his father. Bernger sent him stumbling away with a punch to the nose.

'Talk,' Roald ordered Goswin. He pointed at the enraged Notker. 'Talk or I'll let the priest loose.'

Goswin nodded. 'I'll tell. Notker came here to remove the protective wards, the seals that were left by the Stormcasts when the old von Koeterbergs helped them take the fortress from the barbarians.'

'Of course,' Lothar said. 'Sigmar's crusaders would ensure that any lingering traces of Chaos could do no harm. The right wards would have sanctified Mhurghast, inoculated the castle, as it were, against corruption.' He directed a withering look at Notker. 'To remove such protection would be necessary to summon a daemon. It would need a priest – or a man who had been a priest – to effectively commit such blasphemy.'

Notker stopped struggling against his captors. He hung his head in shame. 'I didn't know why the count wanted the wards removed. It was fifteen years ago and I was desperate for money. The count paid me well.'

'You knew it could only be for some malignant purpose that someone would ask for such a thing,' Roald said. 'A priest above anyone else would know this!'

'I thought...' Notker looked over to where Reiner stood with his hand across his face and blood streaming from his nose. 'I thought the count was trying to use magic to speak with his son's spirit. After the way I'd failed Hagen, I felt obligated to do what I could. Even if it was blasphemous.'

A scream drowned out whatever else Notker might have said. Roald turned to Inge. She screamed again and pointed a quivering hand towards Reiner. 'His eyes! His eyes!'

In their shock, Bruno and Bernger relaxed their grip on Notker. The old priest broke away from them and rushed to Reiner. He pulled the shielding hand away from his son's face. Then he backed away in stark terror.

'Sigmar's mercy,' Roald swore as he looked upon Reiner's face. The man's nose was a gory mess from Bernger's punch, but it wasn't half as terrible as the eyes. The baron could well understand Inge's scream. The eyes had turned completely crimson. No pupil or iris, just two pools of blood.

'The daemon.' Ottokar backed away from Reiner and grabbed Magda with his good arm, pulling her along with him as he retreated across the room. 'The daemon's inside him.'

Reiner's expression became one of utter horror. He clutched at his face, trying to feel the disfiguration that had provoked such fear. A tremor rushed through him, every muscle in his body writhing in the same instant. Somehow he remained standing as the seizure passed. His face was contorted in an agony of terror. A horrible groan slobbered up from his throat when he tried to speak, a sound that had no kinship to anything human.

'Get him,' Roald ordered. The baron made no move to act upon his own command. Bruno and Bernger started towards Reiner while two of the valets came at him from behind.

'No! It's not me! It's not me!' Reiner shouted in a voice that seemed to claw its way up from some echoing pit. He fled before the advancing Walkenhorsts. In his retreat he collided with one of the valets. A slap from Reiner sent the servant flying as though he'd been kicked by a gargant. He slammed into the parlour wall and slid to the floor, his skull fractured by the impact. A ghastly sob of horror rippled from Reiner's mouth as he looked down in shock at the dead man.

'Don't let him get away!' Roald thundered. It was already too late. Only the servants stood between Reiner and the hallway. After what had happened to the valet, none of them dared stand in Reiner's path. They scrambled to step aside as the possessed man hurtled past them and into the castle's dark corridors.

'After him!' Roald pulled Goswin out of the chair and pushed him towards the door. He swept his gaze across the other guests. 'We can't let him get away!'

Hartmann shook his head and sank down onto a divan. 'I'm not going to chase after that thing.' He nodded at the trembling Notker. 'It's his problem. If his son is possessed, the daemon will come looking for him, not me.'

Bruno glared at the merchant. 'You'd sit aside and let that happen? Let his own son come back to kill him?'

'Right now the daemon is weak,' Lothar said. 'It has not completely taken over its host. It is vulnerable.'

'On your feet,' Roald ordered. 'We have to get Reiner before he can–'

Inge cried out and rushed over to the baron. 'You can't kill him! You mustn't!' Her eyes were imploring Roald. When she found no sympathy there, she looked to Hiltrude for support. 'Don't you understand? If you kill Reiner the daemon will seek out another host! Another of our children!'

'She's right,' Lothar said. 'If we kill the host, only the host dies. The daemon will prevail.'

Alrik slammed his fist into his palm. 'Then we just catch him. Catch him and lock him up so the daemon can't get out.'

Roald nodded in agreement. 'Find Reiner and catch him,' he told the rest. 'Under no circumstances must he be harmed.'

'We can search a larger area if we split up,' Thilo suggested.

'The servants know the castle better than any of us,' Bernger said, pointing to them. They were just inside the parlour now, talking in lowered voices with Goswin. The menials seemed uncertain whether to stay or withdraw into the corridor.

'You there,' Roald snapped at them. 'Your lives are in jeopardy as much as ours are. Help us find Reiner and we may be able to get that mob to let us leave Mhurghast.' He felt his temper fray when his speech was met with sullen stares. 'It wasn't a request,' he said. Roald began splitting the servants and the guests into small hunting parties, each charged with a different section of the castle.

'Someone should stay with the aelf,' Hartmann suggested, pointing at the still senseless Abarahm.

'My wife can look after him,' Lothar said. He motioned to the listless Saskia and guided her over to the aelf. She sat beside him with detached indifference, barely glancing at her charge.

'There is another problem,' Lothar told Roald. He indicated Notker, who was almost as listless as the alchemist's wife.

'He may as well stay here,' Roald said. 'He is no good to anyone this way.'

'You'd be wrong there.' Alrik pulled at his long beard as he continued. 'Seems to me that whoever takes the priest along stands a good chance of findin' his son.'

Alrik laid his hand on Notker's shoulder and guided him to join the group the duardin was leading. 'You see, the rest of you will just be lookin' for the daemon. But us... With the priest along... well, while we're lookin' for it, it'll be lookin' for *us*.'

The halls of Mhurghast felt as though they were closing in around Magda, tightening around her like the coil of a noose. The servants were lighting each lamp and candle they passed as their group navigated the dark corridors, but illumination did little to offset the gloom. The dark iron walls sucked all the warmth from the light, leaving it as chill as grave-wisps flickering over a cemetery.

Magda berated herself for her morbid imaginings. The situation was dire enough without populating the castle with phantoms. Her fingers tightened around the old falchion she'd removed from a display in one of the hallways. It was a heavy, clumsy sword compared to the weapons her father made, but there was something reassuring in its solidity. The daemon Count Wulfsige had summoned might be a fiend of blackest Chaos, but Reiner was flesh and blood. He could be killed, if it came to that.

She could see her father up ahead, following close behind the footman and maid who were guiding their group through the castle. Ottokar had thrown aside the rich coat he'd worn to dinner and had shifted the scabbard of his sword around so that he could draw it more easily with his left hand. On those occasions when he kept away from the bottle, the swordsmith was blindingly fast. This was such an occasion. She couldn't remember ever seeing him with such intense focus, such steely determination in his eyes.

Magda started forwards to join her father, but the soft touch of Inge's hand on her shoulder held her back. 'Leave him,' her mother said. 'He wants to find Reiner first, so that if anything happens we'll have time to get away.'

'He has to know I wouldn't leave him,' Magda said. She gestured back to the rest of their group. Hartmann already looked ready to bolt, with or without his family. It was evident from the way the Senfs carried the weapons they'd taken from the suits of armour in the hall that none of them knew how or cared to use them. 'Somebody has to help.'

A sad smile appeared on Inge's face. 'I think he's depending on me to make you leave.' She leaned on the spear she'd armed herself with. 'There isn't much trust between us. All of that went away a very long time ago.'

'Was it when you were with Bruno Walkenhorst?' Magda asked, thinking of the accusation the count had made.

Colour rushed into Inge's cheeks, anger flaring in her eyes.

For a moment it seemed she wasn't going to answer. But then an air of defeat settled over her. No, not defeat, but something Magda had thought Inge incapable of. Regret.

Inge sighed. 'Bruno was long before I met your father,' she said. 'I was dazzled by him, his dashing swagger, his boldness and bravery. I met him through Hagen. They were friends, you see. Good friends.' She scowled and shook her head. 'The count was wrong. Bruno did not come between me and his son. Hagen did. He started to change, became obsessed with rebuilding the von Koeterberg fortune. He was trying to measure up, to prove himself to Count Wulfsige. He began to gamble, and then to take out loans to cover his losses. As his debts mounted, he sought to ease the turmoil in his mind. That's when Lothar Krebs and his vile potions must have taken hold of him. The man I had known, the Hagen who had courted me, started to vanish, replaced by this weak, miserable stranger I didn't know. So I sought comfort elsewhere. There was already a connection between myself and Bruno.

'It didn't last. Hagen discovered us. There was a fight between him and Bruno, a fight that Bruno won.' Tears appeared in Inge's eyes as she recalled that long-ago scene. 'There was such a look on Hagen's face when Bruno knocked the sword from his hand. It was a look of ultimate loss, an expression that did not simply welcome death, but demanded it! He called on Bruno to kill him. I can still hear his terrible words. "You have taken all that is valuable to me. Now take what I have no use for." Bruno refused and did his best to explain, but Hagen would hear none of it. The next day we learned he was dead. Even then we knew the count's story was a lie. That Hagen had taken his own life. That knowledge killed the love between us. In less than a fortnight we had gone our separate ways.'

'Does Father know?' Magda asked.

Inge shrugged. 'I suspect he does. Perhaps not all the details, but enough to be close to the truth.' There was an appeal in her gaze when she looked at Magda, begging her to understand. 'After Bruno... and Hagen... I wasn't so demure as I had been. Ottokar was simply another man of the moment, of no special...'

Magda's eyes widened with shock. 'Mother, you–'

'I have remained with him many years now,' Inge said, firmness in her voice. 'Neither of us would say there is any deep feeling between us. Whatever you may think of me, do not neglect to give your father his share.'

'Then why do you stay?' Magda demanded. 'Why perpetuate such a farce?'

'Because we have one thing in common. One thing that binds us as closely as though we were in the same skin.' Inge nodded down the corridor to where Ottokar was peering into a room the footman had opened for him. 'The one trust we share between us. It's our love for you that keeps us together. That's why he trusts me to keep you safe.'

Magda frowned. 'Then neither of you understands me at all,' she said. Before her mother could try to stop her, she marched down to the open door and slipped into the room Ottokar had entered. The footman stepped aside as Magda passed him.

The room was long and narrow, dominated by a broad table that stood in its centre. High-backed chairs of copper and ash lined the walls. Racks of ivory balls hung above the chairs, each of them marked with a different rune. The table itself was pockmarked with little holes, each designated with the same runes. Magda was only vaguely familiar with the game of *maharal*, a pastime brought to Ravensbach by settlers from Azyr. She was certain, however, that there shouldn't be a large, cloth-draped mass stretched across the centre of the game table.

Ottokar stood beside it, his hand closed about his sword. 'Pull back the sheet,' he said. He blinked in surprise when he saw Magda instead of the footman come forwards to carry out the order.

Magda didn't give Ottokar the chance to send her back. Her fingers closed on the edge of the sheet and whipped it back. She gasped at what was revealed. Count Wulfsige's body, his throat slashed so deeply that she could see bone.

'The servants said this was where they took their master,' Ottokar said. His gaze was sharp when he looked at Magda. 'What would you have done if it was Reiner under there? If the daemon had chosen this spot to hide?'

'What would you have done?' Magda threw the question back at him. She pointed at the footman, who had withdrawn into the hall and was peeking in through the doorway. 'I doubt he'd have been any help.' She saw the frustration in her father's face as he struggled to refute her logic.

'Well, it's obvious Reiner isn't hiding here,' Ottokar decided after looking around the room.

Magda didn't respond. Instead she went back to the game table and took a closer look at the corpse. Something was wrong. It took her a moment to realise what. When she did, she reached across the table and pushed the count's body, trying to prop it up on its side.

'Whatever are you doing?' Inge asked as she walked into the room. Hartmann and his family chased after her like a string of ducklings. Once they spotted the corpse, however, they decided to linger near the doorway.

'You'll have to ask your daughter,' Ottokar retorted. 'I can't see what's provoked her.'

Magda turned and faced her parents. 'That weird knife he used to cut his throat,' she said. 'They took it away with him, but it isn't here.'

'You must be mistaken then,' Hartmann suggested. 'I think I remember seeing it in the dining hall.'

'No, Magda's right,' Inge said. 'The valets did take the knife when they removed the body.'

'Then that means someone's been here.' Magda tapped her fingers on the table. 'Someone came here and took the knife.'

'The daemon.' Inge shuddered, her voice low. 'It was here. It came for the knife.'

Ottokar shook his head. 'What would a daemon want with a knife? There has been plenty of opportunity for almost anyone to slip in here and take it.'

'But the same question – why would someone want it?' Magda asked.

Before anyone could offer an answer, Sigune Senf cried out. Everyone turned to see her waving frantically and pointing out into the hallway.

'The servants!' Sigune yelled. 'They're gone! They've left us!'

Bernger swung the huge mace against the lock, battering its mechanism with all the strength he could muster. He could feel the oak door shudder under the impact, but it stubbornly held fast.

'Those treacherous dogs are getting away!' Roald shouted.

Bernger didn't waste breath snapping back at the baron. None of them should have taken their eyes off Goswin and the valets. Roald's presumption made it impossible for him to consider that the servants might be anything but servile, but the rest of them should have known better. Even Hiltrude hadn't let her noble rank dull her common sense. But Bernger knew he'd let his own wariness be lulled by Roald's assumption of authority. It was a mistake he would never have made under other conditions.

'A few more hits should break it,' Bernger said as he smashed the lock again. Bruno stood nearby with his sword unsheathed, ready to lunge out into the corridor. Roald had a blade of his own, a rakish thing he'd claimed from a crystal case in one of the hallways. Hiltrude and Liebgarde had only a couple of knives, and accepting even that much weaponry had required harsh words from Bruno.

'They must be mad,' Hiltrude said. 'Leading us into this conservatory and then locking the door behind us.'

Bruno shook his head. 'Not so mad if there's another way out of Mhurghast.'

Roald sneered at the idea. 'They would be fools then. Surely they know they would be richly rewarded if they got us out of this godsforsaken castle.'

'Goswin probably knows a lot about what the count was up to,' Bruno said. 'If he took any of us out of here, he might be taking the daemon along too. Whatever you paid him, a dead man couldn't spend it.'

The lock shuddered as Bernger smashed it again. The door groaned in its iron frame. He stepped back and brought his shoulder slamming into its panels. What was left of the lock flew apart, bouncing across the tile floor. Bernger burst out into the hallway. He thought he heard someone running down the stairs at the far end of the corridor.

'Someone went down that way,' he told his father as Bruno joined him in the hall.

'It could be another trick,' Bruno said. He glanced down the dark stretch of passageway that led away from the stairs.

'If we argue they'll get away,' Bernger said. He dashed off towards the stairs while his father shouted back to the von Woernhoers and started for the darkened passage.

Bernger didn't know if Roald and his family would follow either of them. He didn't have time to think about it. The retreating footfalls were growing fainter with every heartbeat. When he reached the stairs he plunged down them with reckless speed, springing down the spiral with bold leaps. He could hear the footsteps growing quicker. Those he was chasing knew they were being pursued.

Bernger hurtled around the last turn of the winding staircase and landed in a crouch on the marble floor. He spun around in the direction he had heard the footsteps. A glimpse of a valet rushing into a hallway was all he needed. From his crouch he threw himself forwards and sprinted after the servant.

The flicker of candlelight illuminated the narrow corridor down which Bernger chased the valet. He was just able to keep the man in sight. When he turned a corner into another passageway, here too there were candles lighting the way. Surely Goswin and the valets had not taken the time to light them all. It dawned on him that the other servants must also be involved. Most of the maids had not been delegated to the search parties. If Goswin had confided in them, they might have gone ahead and ensured the escape route was lit up for the major-domo whenever he could slip away. Perhaps the servants in the other search parties had done the same.

The valet threw open a huge blackwood door, its panels carved with the figures of knights and dragons. He turned to slam it shut in Bernger's face, but must have decided his pursuer was too close. The servant spun back around and ran away.

Bernger flung himself past the open door, heedless of the threat of ambush. No enemy lay in wait for him. The only sign of life was the fleeing valet. The servant was darting around crystal-fronted display cases and magnificently decorated suits of armour. The bestial shadows of crouching lashwolves and snarling frostbears leered in stuffed savagery.

Overhead, the preserved pinions of a reptilian ripperhawk hung from the ceiling on golden chains. The valet's retreat led through the trophy hall of the von Koeterbergs – at every turn was exhibited the glories and triumphs of Count Wulfsige's predecessors.

The valet began tearing at the displays he passed. He knocked over suits of armour and upended crystal cases of ancient rings and sacred awards. Anything he could throw into the path of his pursuer. But whatever he tried, Bernger kept on his tail and steadily closed the distance between them. Finally the man summoned a last burst of speed and rushed at a massive standard that covered a stretch of the wall. He grabbed at the lower edge of the cloth and flipped it away. There was an open doorway behind the standard.

Bernger dove in after the valet. There were stairs beyond the doorway, and from the dirt and dust that caked them, he guessed it was a stairwell that was seldom used. Likely some mechanism more substantial than the standard that curtained it off kept the entrance hidden normally. Now, of course, things were far from normal.

The stairs were lost in darkness, the only light coming from the candles in the trophy room and a faint glow from below. Accustomed to working in much darker conditions, Bernger was able to keep his footing on the dusty steps. The valet was not so fortunate. A loud crash sounded from ahead, followed by a painful outburst. Bernger reached the servant as he recovered from his fall. Before the man could run off again, Bernger grabbed him by his collar. The valet started to pull away, but it was not so dark in the stairway that he failed to see the mace in his captor's hand.

'So, tell me what this is all about,' Bernger demanded. He shook the valet.

The servant started to answer. Then an anguished scream

rang out from below. The sound took both men by surprise, but it was the valet's panic that proved the greater. Before Bernger realised what was happening, the man twisted out of his grasp and dove down the steps.

'Stop!' Bernger called out as he chased after the man. He was only a few paces behind the valet when he reached the bottom of the stairs. There was a small landing with walls of iron and a doorway at the other end. It was towards this doorway that the valet ran.

Bernger hurried after him. He was gaining on the servant when the man rushed through the doorway. Some instinct, the inner voice that sometimes warned him of danger when he was pilfering the home of a wealthy burgher, caused Bernger to hang back for an instant just before the threshold.

Beyond the doorway was a wide corridor. The valet was rushing across this, seeking a doorway on the other side. In his haste, it seemed the servant had missed the blood spattered about the floor, and the gory drops that fell from the ceiling. Bernger shouted a warning to the man, but if he heard it was too late.

The floor of the hall was tiled, a mosaic of carved stone blocks. The valet was a little more than halfway across when his foot landed on the wrong tile. There was a growl of moving gears and the rumble of machinery. The servant looked up and uttered a scream very like what they'd heard in the stairway.

From his angle outside the corridor, Bernger could see the ceiling sliding back into the wall, revealing a higher roof, one composed of hundreds of long steel spikes. There were bodies impaled on those spikes, blood dripping from their wounds. Bernger recognised all the victims as servants of the late Count Wulfsige.

The valet tried to run, but it was already too late. Like the descending foot of a gargant, the spikes smashed down and transfixed him. As quickly as it had struck, the murderous roof withdrew back into its place above the corridor and the false ceiling slid across to conceal its presence.

Bernger watched with ghastly appreciation the blood that dripped down through cracks in the ceiling. He heard another sound, however, one that came from beyond the trapped corridor. Footsteps. Somebody had made it across

His stomach felt as though it was going to crawl up his throat and choke him when Bernger started past the doorway and into the corridor. He studied the floor intently, especially the spot where the valet had triggered his doom. There were subtle variations in the tiles, but it was not the designs that he considered important. Some of them were slightly raised, a fraction of an inch higher than the others. One of these suspicious tiles was where the valet had been standing when the machinery started.

Doubt assailed Bernger. If he was wrong, he would be inviting a hideous death. But if he was right... if he was right, he might have found another way out of the castle. The ancient von Koeterbergs had shown the Stormcasts a secret way into Mhurghast. Perhaps this was it.

The sound of someone exerting themselves from somewhere ahead goaded Bernger on. It could be some of the servants striving to open a secret exit.

Slowly, his pulse sounding like thunder in his ears, Bernger walked towards the danger spot. He avoided the tile he had noted and took another step. There was no rumble of machinery. The ceiling remained in place, hiding the deadly spikes. His confidence bolstered, Bernger pressed on. He carefully navigated the raised tiles and finally reached the further doorway.

Here he found a short landing. It made a sharp turn to

the left and opened into a narrow, copper-floored hallway. Instantly three things impressed themselves on Bernger's senses. The first was the hideous heat that emanated from the glowing metal walls that flanked the hallway. The second was the abominable stench of burnt flesh that boiled off the charred bodies seared against those same walls. The third was the lone figure slowly creeping across the copper floor. Goswin reached the doorway at the other side while Bernger watched. The major-domo turned around and gave him a malicious smile.

'None of you will leave this castle,' he gloated. 'The count's revenge will claim all of you!'

Bernger waved his mace at Goswin. 'There's a way out,' he said. 'That's how you got these poor devils to follow you.' He gestured at the charred bodies cooking on the heated walls.

'They were not agile enough,' Goswin said. 'Perhaps you can do better.'

Bernger knew Goswin was trying to coax him into something reckless. He wasn't about to play the major-domo's game. Warily, he put one foot out onto the copper floor. It waved and wobbled under his step. Far from being as solid as it appeared, the floor was simply a thin sheet that warped under a person's weight and would toss them towards the red-hot walls.

Goswin laughed when Bernger pulled his foot back. 'Now you know how it works. Are you brave enough to try?' He laughed again. 'I won't wait for you. I'm going to press ahead. Maybe I'll destroy the door once I'm away. Wouldn't that be amusing?'

The major-domo slipped from view, still laughing at Bernger's predicament. He saw Goswin move to one side and judged there must be another doorway and another corridor hidden from his view. For a little while, he could still hear Goswin laughing. Then there was the snarl of some mechanism stirring to life. The laugh rose into a wail of terror that was abruptly silenced.

Goswin had successfully navigated two of Count Wulfsige's traps, but it was clear that there was at least a third. Some murderous implement the major-domo was either unaware of or had forgotten about. Either way, he wouldn't be leaving the castle.

Bernger considered the fiendishness of the traps he had seen and however many others stood between them and escape. The cruel choice left to them by the vengeful Count Wulfsige. To brave the horrors of the castle's dungeons or the daemon that stalked its halls.

CHAPTER V

It was Sigune's suggestion that brought Magda's group to Mhurghast's chapel. Tall and narrow, if anything the place had an even gloomier atmosphere than the rest of the castle. Dust caked the altar and covered the marble hammer that was bolted to the wall. Silvery cobwebs stretched across the beams overhead, fitfully reflecting the light from the gilded braziers Inge and Sigune ignited. The dried wood gave off a musty smell as it burned, somehow making the dereliction of the place even more pronounced.

Magda prowled between the decrepit pews. They were carved from a silvery sort of wood that she had never seen before, with intricate engravings that depicted the great constellations and the twin-tailed Comet of Sigmar. The legs of each bench were rendered into the clawed foot of Dracothion, and at each end of the pews was a carved support representing the winged dragon. Soft, velvet-covered padding stretched across the seats, and when she set her hand against them she could feel the richness of the material even under the patina of grime.

Windows opened out from either side of the altar, massive arches filled with panels of stained glass. The left side depicted gold-armoured Stormcasts descending upon Chamon in a blast of lightning. A few skin-clad tribesmen were in the foreground as they cautiously approached the mighty knights. The right window showed one of the tribesmen standing with the Stormcasts and pointing at a dark castle atop a craggy hill. Magda recognised the fortress as Mhurghast and reasoned that the tribesman must be the scion of the von Koeterbergs who had aided the holy warriors in seizing the castle from the barbarians that held it. She was impressed by the attentive workmanship, the adoration of the artist evident in each line and figure. The effect was inspiring even in darkness. She could only imagine how much more magnificent it must be with daylight streaming through it.

'This is certainly the best place to be,' Hartmann was telling his son and daughter. 'Your mother is quite right. A daemon wouldn't dare enter a place sanctified to the God-King.' The merchant and his children sat in one of the pews, poised so that they could see out through the iron gate that opened into the chapel. The younger Senfs appeared unconvinced by their father's assurances. From his nervousness and the way he was sweating, Hartmann did not seem especially convinced either. It would appear Sigune had all the faith in their household.

Magda watched Sigune for a moment as she walked through the chapel, lighting the braziers. She had a strange sort of confidence in her expression, given the circumstances. Frequently she would pause to look up at the altar and the hammer suspended above it. It was easy enough to guess the source of her strength. Faith in Sigmar's power, the conviction that all things happened in accordance with the God-King's design.

That kind of faith was something Magda had never known. It wasn't that she didn't believe in Sigmar's power or that she failed to venerate Him. It was simply an appreciation of the cold fact that Sigmar didn't rule alone. There were other gods, some of them dire and baleful. They too had their domains and their influence upon the lives of mortals. How far the protection of one god could extend into the dominion of another was a puzzle scholars and priests tirelessly debated without reaching a consensus. If such learned people couldn't resolve such a question, who was Magda to believe she had the answers?

Often she had met Klueger in temples and shrines devoted to Sigmar. This chapel felt different. Certainly all the expected holy designs were here, the images of the Hammer and the Comet, the sacred appeals to Sigmar carved in stone above the nave. But there was something absent, something that wasn't seen but rather felt. A feeling of welcome and protection that simply wasn't here.

Magda shuddered when she considered that absence. Was it something about this place, or was it something else? Something inside her. She had eaten the profaned food and thereby drawn into herself the mark of Khorne. Did that mean she was now corrupt? Irrevocably damned? Did the chapel feel different to her because she had fallen outside Sigmar's domain? She wished Klueger were here. He would know the answers.

A feeling of horror coursed through Magda. Klueger would know, but what would he know? What if the answer was indeed that she was irrevocably damned! Doomed to be consumed by Chaos, to fall into the infernal grasp of Khorne. What would Klueger do then? She had often heard him describe the severity of his vocation, the harsh lengths to which the Order of Azyr had to go to protect people from the Dark Gods. The witch hunters could permit no trace of corruption to escape. Perhaps that now meant Magda. Suddenly she hoped nobody got word to Klueger. It was terrible enough to think about the daemon, but it was even worse to think Klueger might be the one who had to kill her.

Magda moved across the chapel to join Inge. She needed someone to talk to, to get her mind away from the grim fears she had started to dwell on. Her father had gone to the parlour to bring Saskia and Abarahm back to the chapel. She would have preferred to talk to him. Inge was less than sympathetic to her relationship with Klueger. Before, Magda had always imagined Inge's reservations to be a reflection of her own unrealised social ambitions. Now she wasn't so sure. She'd had to rethink several of her preconceptions about her parents this night. Maybe her mother's reservations had more to do with Klueger's being a witch hunter, a man to be feared as well as respected. A man who would suffer no evil, even for the sake of those who loved him.

Inge had left the last two braziers on the right side of the chapel unlit. When Magda walked over to her, she was kneeling beside a marble sarcophagus. The cover was sculpted into the life-size image of a young man with his hands crossed over his chest. The face was quite vividly depicted and the resemblance to Count Wulfsige left Magda in no doubt whose remains were within.

'I always suspected,' Inge said when she sensed her daughter standing behind her. 'I never bothered to find out for sure. Perhaps I was afraid to.'

Magda took Inge's hand in her own. 'Would it have changed anything? What good would it have done to know how Hagen died?'

Inge set her other hand on the cold stone. 'Maybe nothing. Maybe everything.' She turned and looked at the carved face. 'That was how he looked before... before the decline. Strong but sensitive, always with a kind of hidden smile he'd try to restrain until he had no choice but to release it in an absurd grin. He was so vibrant, so determined. He had to succeed on his own, you see. He was too proud of his heritage to merely accept a legacy. He felt compelled to build his own.

'Do you know he refused a commission in the Freeguild? As the count's son he had no business marching with the rank and file. But he did. That was the kind of man he was.' A sad smile pulled at Inge's face. 'I think that was why he was so set on having me. Not some lady from the noble houses, coaxed and groomed by the count's influence. He wanted someone he felt he had earned on his own, had won through his own work. That was the big contention between Hagen and the count. It was what caused Hagen to push too hard, to reach too fast. He had to prove himself.'

Magda knelt beside Inge. 'That was his choice. It wasn't your fault.'

'It was, you know,' Inge said. 'It all started with me, and it all ended with me too. The deeper Hagen sank, the less love I had for him. The less he had for me, too, I think. By the end I believe I was nothing to him but a trophy, something to show the count and justify himself.' She stood and looked down at the stone face. 'Somewhere along the way, Hagen forgot his pride and his integrity. All that mattered was to win. To be right. When he couldn't have me, he couldn't have his victory, couldn't show the count that he was his own man. Rather than live with that, Hagen chose to die.'

'Hagen made that choice,' Magda said, standing to face her mother. 'Nobody could make it for him. The man you describe, the man you loved, wasn't the same man you left. You know that.'

Inge drew Magda close to her. 'What I know is that this terrible thing threatens us because of what I did. If I'd only–'

'If you'd done anything different, I wouldn't be here anyway,' Magda said, cutting her off. 'You wouldn't have married father and I wouldn't have been born.' She turned her mother around and nodded towards Hartmann. 'Even the count knew you weren't entirely to blame. That's why he spread his vengeance among all these people.'

Hartmann suddenly got to his feet. He scrambled back, leaving his children in the pew. The merchant cast his frightened gaze around the chapel until he spotted Magda. He knew she was the only real fighter in their little group. 'I hear someone outside in the hallway,' he said as he continued to retreat deeper into the room. 'They sound like they're coming this way.'

Magda shook her head at the merchant's unreasoning fright. 'If you hear more than one person, then it can't be the...' She hesitated, unwilling to name the thing they all feared. 'It can't be Reiner.'

'Maybe... maybe the daemon found friends,' Hartmann suggested as he climbed the few steps up to the altar. He gave Sigune a panicked look. 'You don't know. It might have friends.'

Magda walked towards the gate, her mother following close behind her with the spear. The Senf children joined Hartmann up at the altar while Sigune dashed across the chapel to light the last braziers.

As ridiculous as Hartmann's idea about the daemon bringing friends was, Magda felt uneasy when she heard lowered voices approaching the chapel. It was only when she recognised Roald's acid tones that she started to relax. A moment later she heard Ottokar respond to him, and the last of her concern dripped away.

'It's father,' Magda told the others. 'He's coming back.' Inge set down the spear and helped her move the pew they'd dragged over to block the gate. Once it was aside, they pulled the iron bars inwards and opened a path for Ottokar and the others.

The swordsmith had done more than simply collect Saskia and the aelf. He also had Roald's group with him. At least, that was Magda's initial impression, but as they filed into the chapel, she noticed that the servants who'd been with Roald were gone. Then she realised that Bernger was also missing.

Roald stopped just inside the gateway and quickly scrutinised the chapel. 'I approve,' he said. 'This sanctuary should be the best place in the castle to guard ourselves against a daemon.'

'Then you didn't find Reiner either?' Inge asked.

'Those treacherous servants deserted us the same as they did you,' Roald declared. 'Rather than stumble about in the dark, we thought it prudent to return to the parlour. We were just in time to join Ottokar to come over here.'

'What about the duardin and Lothar?' Magda looked over at Bruno. 'And where is Bernger?'

Bruno shook his head. 'We saw no sign of Alrik and his group. Even if the servants with him disappear, they still have Notker to guide them.' His expression became grave. 'As for Bernger, we split up to try and catch Goswin and the valets when they ran off. I didn't catch anyone. Maybe he did.'

Roald stiffened at Bruno's tone. 'You have no idea where Bernger went. It would be idiocy to go prowling the castle looking for him. The smart thing to do is stay here. There is always strength in numbers.'

Magda felt her blood boil at Roald's sneering tone. 'If it was your daughter missing, would you stay here?'

Hiltrude smiled as she led Liebgarde past Roald and towards

one of the pews. 'He would not be so callous as to sit back and do nothing. Oh, he would not go himself, you understand, but he would send somebody to search.'

'We can defend ourselves better if we have more capable swordsmen here,' Roald stated as he scowled at Hiltrude.

Magda nodded to the baron. 'Then you won't miss me. I'll go and find Bernger.'

Ottokar stepped between Magda and the hall, while Inge moved over to her side. 'The baron might not miss you, but we would,' her father said. 'You aren't going.'

Magda started to protest, but Bruno was making his own case to Roald.

'You've just explained why someone has to go,' Bruno said. 'Since we didn't find the... Reiner, our chances are better if we keep together. I'll find Bernger and Alrik's group and bring them back here.'

Hartmann came running over from the altar. 'Not Notker!' he told Bruno. 'You won't bring him here! He's the one the daemon will be looking for!'

Magda rounded on the merchant. 'He has just as much a right to survive as you do.'

'Besides,' Bruno added. 'The man *was* a priest. He might have some idea about how to fend off this thing. Certainly he'd know how best to protect ourselves in this sanctuary.'

'Just go and find them,' Roald said. 'Since you are so intent, get it over with.' The baron's hard gaze swept across the other guests. 'But this is it. We won't send anyone to look for you if you do not come back.'

Bruno nodded in agreement and started for the gate. Before he left, he smiled at Magda. 'Thank you for volunteering, but I have to do this. Bernger's my son.'

'I understand,' Magda replied. 'Sigmar watch over you,' she added as Bruno headed off down the hallway. Ottokar closed the gate behind him while Hartmann and his son, Heimo, dragged the pew back over to block the entrance.

Magda turned and looked back at the altar and the golden hammer behind it. 'Sigmar watch over all of us,' she prayed.

Even in this holy place, the words felt hollow.

The dark halls of Mhurghast felt more desolate than ever when Bernger returned from the dungeons and their grisly traps. Just knowing the murderous devices were down there was like a black stain in his mind. The carnage they'd wrought on the servants was something that gnawed at him, a horror that shivered in his very soul. He wondered what had befallen Goswin, whether the major-domo's death had been quick or slow. It was hard to dredge up any sympathy for the man, but even so his final scream continued to haunt Bernger.

The castle's corridors were utterly silent as Bernger stole through them. There was something bitterly ironic about the dark quiet. When he was prowling through the homes and businesses of Ravensbach, such conditions would have been cheered by him and his fellow thieves. Now he felt as he imagined the victims of his intrusions must have felt. He appreciated the unknown menace that lay behind the lurking dark and the ponderous silence.

Somewhere, waiting in the dark, perhaps just around the next bend, was Reiner. Or at least the thing that had been Reiner. Bernger wondered what would happen if he were to stumble upon the daemon now, alone. Even if the monster's prey was supposed to be Notker, he doubted it would be so discreet as to restrict itself to a single victim.

Bernger raised his mace as he stepped around a corner. There was a dark shape there, poised against the wall. He swung the heavy bludgeon at it, striking for its head. He felt a ringing impact as he smashed the thing. A loud clatter echoed down the hall as the suit of armour fell to the floor and some of its components went spinning free from the armature that held it together.

Bernger sighed as he stepped over the wreckage. Not for the first time he remonstrated with himself for getting turned around and losing track of the candles the servants had left. Now he was simply stumbling around in the dark, trying to at least find some part of the castle that he recognised.

He'd walked only a few yards from the armour when he thought he saw a light at the far end of the corridor. It was gone so quickly that he wondered if he'd seen it at all. His first thought was Reiner, but if the daemon was fully in control of him now, would it even need a light to guide it through the castle? Then Bernger wondered if it could be one of the servants, someone who'd got lost on their way to the trophy room. If so, then they had no idea what was waiting for them in the dungeons.

Bernger quickened his pace and jogged down the corridor towards where he'd seen the light. He rejected the impulse to call out. Even if whoever had the light was friendly, there was no knowing what else might be listening.

Halfway down the corridor, Bernger became aware of movement in the dark ahead of him. It was crouched low, but moving at a good pace. More than that he couldn't see, but it was enough to bring him up short and have him make ready with the mace.

'None of that, lad,' a gruff whisper sliced through the silence. The voice came from ahead, where he'd spotted movement.

'Alrik?' Bernger whispered back.

A low laugh replied. 'Close. I'm Brond Alriksson.' Another grunt of amusement. 'I keep forgettin' you manlings are as blind as burrow-worms in the dark.'

Bernger knew from experience how sharp a duardin's eyes

were. Some of them made a good living as night guards for Ravensbach's nobles.

'Are you alone?' he asked.

'No. My father's back down there with the alchemist and the rest,' Brond said. 'Your father's with them. He persuaded us to go looking for you. We'd already been this way though. Would have passed you by if you didn't knock something over.'

'A suit of armour. In the dark I thought it was Reiner.'

'I'm not too proud to say we'd the same idea when we heard the racket. My father blew out the light and I came down here to see what was what.' Brond muttered a duardin oath. 'Suits me that it is you and not Reiner.'

'You haven't seen him? Is Notker still with you?'

'Aye, but those cussed servants lit out. Your father tells us the ones with the other groups also took off. Thinks they knew some secret way out of the castle.'

Bernger's blood felt cold when he answered Brond. 'They thought so,' he said, then went on to describe what he'd seen in the dungeon.

Silence ensued. For some reason, it seemed some sort of tension had imposed itself between Bernger and Brond. Finally the duardin spoke. 'I'd better lead you to the others. Your father will be happy to see you. Keep your hand on my shoulder until we get there.'

The duardin's rough hand closed on Bernger's and guided his fingers to Brond's shoulder. Bernger had to stoop somewhat as he followed him down the hall, but he was impressed by how quickly the duardin navigated in the dark. The idle thought came to him that if a few like Brond became thieves they'd be able to pick Ravensbach clean in a fortnight.

'I'm back,' Brond whispered when they reached the end of the hall. 'We can stop lookin' for Bruno's boy. He's with me.'

Light flared up as Lothar removed the lead cover from

the lantern he was carrying. Beside him was his son, Thilo, an old sabre tucked under his belt. Alrik had purloined an ugly-looking mattock from somewhere, the sledge resting over one shoulder as he welcomed Brond back.

Bruno stepped forwards and embraced Bernger, relief on his face. 'I thought I'd lost you.'

'You aren't getting rid of me so easily,' Bernger said. 'But I wouldn't spend too much time looking for the servants.' He was a bit less frank in describing the traps in Mhurghast's dungeon than he had been with Brond. It wouldn't do to worry his father needlessly now that the danger had passed.

At least that particular danger.

Notker came forwards and spoke once Bernger was finished. 'Then they are all dead. If one of them had got away, maybe they would have had pity on us, done something to help us. But they're all dead.'

Alrik frowned at the priest. 'It does no good hopin' for help. You want to save your skin, you do it yourself.' Like with Brond, Bernger felt there was a tension in the cogsmith after he had heard about the dungeon.

'We could help ourselves by leaving him here.' Thilo pointed at Notker. 'Why drag him around and draw Reiner to us?'

'You'd prefer to let Reiner kill him?' Lothar snapped at his son. 'Then the daemon finds a new host for itself.' He tapped his finger against Thilo's chest. 'Maybe next time it takes you, sends you to kill me.'

Bruno also came to Notker's defence. 'The count wanted us to turn on each other. If we stick together, if we fight this thing together, we can beat it.' He turned to the duardin. 'The chapel has only one way in, a gate with iron bars. We'll be able to see Reiner if he tries to get in. Maybe we can fight him from behind the bars. Spears, swords, whatever it takes. Keep fighting him. Keep him from ever getting in.'

Alrik nodded. 'So you still want to use Notker as bait,' he stated. He shifted the weight of the mattock on his shoulders. 'Well, let's go have a look at this chapel and then see what kind of trap we can set.'

The cogsmith had winced when he said *trap*, something that wasn't lost on the humans who heard him. For the moment, however, no one challenged him about it. Bernger suspected that they were of much the same mind as he was. Somewhere in the vastness of Mhurghast, Reiner was prowling the halls, and wherever he was, he would eventually come looking for Notker.

An iron gate and the holy protection of Sigmar sounded like good things to have between themselves and the daemon.

Magda paced behind the iron gate and cast frequent glances through the bars into the darkened hall. Ottokar and Bruno had lit some of the candles when Bruno had left, but as yet there'd been no hint of activity beyond a few rats slinking around.

Ottokar sat in the barricading pew and watched his daughter. Inge was resting in one of the other pews, reluctantly surrendering to her husband's theory that at least one of them should get some sleep.

'Worrying won't make them show up any faster,' Ottokar told Magda.

She stopped pacing and looked at the swordsmith. 'Have you ever tried *not* to think about something?'

Ottokar nodded in defeat. He rapped the hollow silver of his false arm. 'Every day. It doesn't work. The more you try to ignore some things, the more you think about them.'

Magda held her father's gaze. She wanted to talk to him about it, to ask what had happened. He'd never told her before. Not really told her. Everything she knew was bits and pieces picked up here and there. She thought if she asked this time, he would tell her everything. That was why she didn't ask. It might be better not to know.

'Do you think Reiner will come?' she said. 'I mean here, to this sanctuary?'

'Not until it gets Notker,' Ottokar said. He stared off, no longer looking at Magda but at some image in his mind. Something too terrible for words. 'The count said it'd look for a new host once it... did what it was going to do.'

Magda leaned down beside Ottokar and laid her hand on his knee. 'If what happened to Reiner happens to me...'

Ottokar took hold of her and crushed her against him. 'Sigmar's grace, don't say that. Don't even dare to think it! Nothing is going to happen to you. Nothing!'

Sounds from the hallway caused Magda to pull away from her father. She cried out in joy when she saw Bernger and Bruno coming back with the other guests. Her shouts brought the others in the chapel trickling forwards to watch the approaching group.

'So they still have Notker with them,' Roald observed. 'Reiner still hasn't come for him.'

'Maybe... maybe there is no... maybe it isn't real,' Hartmann muttered. 'Maybe it's all just some cruel trick. Maybe Reiner went crazy, had some kind of fit!'

Abarahm rose from the pew Saskia had laid him out on. The aelf's laugh was malicious. 'You can believe whatever idiocy you like, but the count did not wait twenty years and slit his own throat simply to play a trick.'

Hartmann wilted under the aelf's scorn. He withdrew towards the altar, where Sigune continued to offer prayers.

Ottokar and Heimo helped Magda move the blockade. Roald took hold of the gate and regarded the approaching group.

'I will allow the rest of you to enter, but not Notker,' the baron declared. 'He stays outside.'

Magda spun around and glared at him. 'What gives you the right?'

'Rank and breeding.' Roald sneered at her. 'Things your common blood wouldn't appreciate.' He tightened his hold on the gate. 'I'm in command here, and I say that man doesn't enter.'

Roald did not back away, even when Magda's fingers closed around the grip of her falchion. It was when Hiltrude approached him that his swagger vanished.

'If rank and breeding are the measure we are using,' the baroness stated, 'then I would remind you that in our alliance, you are the junior partner.' Hiltrude waved at the gate. 'Open it. Let them in. *All* of them.'

Roald hesitated just a moment too long for Magda's liking. She stepped past him and seized the gate, pulling it from his grip. Roald withdrew, casting dark looks at anyone who glanced his way.

Bernger and Bruno escorted Notker into the chapel. They stepped aside while the others entered. Lothar and Thilo went over to Saskia while the two duardin examined the gateway and began discussing how best to reinforce it.

Magda joined the two Walkenhorsts. 'I talked with my mother. She explained everything. She felt guilty about what happened to Hagen, but I don't think it was her fault.' She laid her hand on Bruno's arm. 'I don't think it was your fault either.'

Bruno shook his head. 'Fault and blame are hard things to accept and even harder to let go of. Hagen made mistakes, but we helped him make them.'

'I talked with my mother beside Hagen's sepulchre–'

'His what?' Notker asked.

Magda pointed to the stone sarcophagus near the altar. 'Hagen's buried there.'

'He can't be,' Notker muttered. 'I didn't allow it.' He walked towards the sarcophagus, mumbling under his breath.

'But there's a sepulchre there,' Magda said.

'Maybe,' Bruno conceded, 'but he can't be inside. Hagen took his own life. His remains would have to be burned and scattered over water to keep his spirit from coming back as a wraith. Count Wulfsige would never have risked that happening to Hagen.'

'But I've seen his sepulchre,' Magda persisted.

Notker was almost at the foot of the steps that climbed up to the altar and the sepulchre beside it. Suddenly there was a furious agitation around the sarcophagus. The heavy stone lid was flung upwards, launched like a boulder from a catapult. It landed among the pews, smashing three rows into kindling. A foul, charnel smell billowed across the sanctuary, the stench of congealed blood. Magda nearly gagged as the reek washed over her. It was an effort to turn her eyes towards the sepulchre. What she saw there turned her blood to ice.

Hagen was not inside the sepulchre, but something else was. It rose upwards on thin legs, rising and rising until it was so tall it had to bow its head to keep from striking the ceiling. Crimson bones showed through the wet, dripping meat of its body, and when it reached out with its skeletal arms, the flesh peeled back in bloody tatters. The head that turned and fixed Notker with its murderous stare was devoid of skin, a huge and fanged skull with hellish fires blazing from its sockets.

'Reiner!' Notker clutched at his chest and tears fell from his eyes.

Magda screamed. She was not the only one. Terror fairly

dripped off everyone in the chapel. Sigune wailed in an agony of fear and prostrated herself before the altar, her hands waving frantically to make the sign of the Hammer again and again. Hiltrude pushed Liebgarde behind her and backed away towards the gate. Lothar fumbled in his pockets, dislodging strange charms and talismans. Thilo cried out and fell in a faint across one of the pews. The Walkenhorsts and the duardin gripped their weapons, but stood frozen in horror at the sight before their eyes.

'The daemon!' Roald shouted. 'You see! I warned you!'

The daemon turned its grisly stare away from Notker and looked towards the altar. Hartmann fled from the dripping monstrosity, running across the chapel until he fell over one of the pews and collapsed to the floor. Sigune screamed. She grabbed the candlesticks from the altar, crying out to Sigmar for protection. In her panic she threw them at the daemon. Even before she did, the bony arms were lifted to ward off the attack. Magda had the ghastly idea that the fiend *knew* what Sigune was going to do even before she did it. The gilded missiles struck the arms and clattered to the floor. The daemon stepped away from the sepulchre and its bony talons closed around Sigune's head. It picked her up and flung her into one of the windows. The stained glass shattered under the impact, but the metal frames held and tossed her back into the chapel, her body shredded by the glass.

'No!' Magda cried. Without thinking about what she was doing, she ran towards the grotesque daemon. Ottokar caught hold of her and spun her around, flinging her into the arms of Bernger and Bruno.

'Hold her!' Ottokar ordered, before drawing his sword and charging towards the sepulchre. Magda struggled against the Walkenhorsts, desperate to break free.

'By the mercy and glory of Sigmar!' Notker was moaning,

his hands closed together and raised towards the daemonic beast in appeal. 'Reiner, have pity on me!'

The daemon glared down at the priest for only a moment, then swung around and glared at the swordsmith as he charged across the chapel. It seemed to relish the man's defiance.

'Father! No!' Magda could only watch as Ottokar put himself between the daemon and Notker. His sword flashed out in the rakish sweep she knew so well. The fiend's belly was opened by the slashing blade. A killing blow, if Ottokar's enemy had been truly alive.

The daemon snatched at Ottokar with one skeletal hand. It caught hold of his fake arm and crushed the hollow limb in its murderous grip. The swordsmith thrust at the daemon, his blade taking it between the ribs. Rancid blood spurted from the wound, but still the monster ignored its hurt. It pulled, and the silver arm ripped away as its straps snapped. Suddenly seizing Ottokar's real arm, the daemon swung him around and bashed him against the altar. A sickening crunch sounded from the impact as his spine folded around the unyielding stone.

The brutal, hideous deaths stunned those who watched. Magda fell to her knees, all the strength drawn out of her when she saw her father die. She could see her mother sitting in open-mouthed horror in one of the pews, paralysed by the havoc around her.

After Ottokar's death, no one made a move when the daemon turned towards Notker again. Least of all the former priest. He was staring up at the death that loomed over him. His gaze was not fixed on the fanged skull or the skeletal talons. Instead he was looking at the tattered rags that clung to the giant daemon. All that remained of the clothes Reiner had been wearing when the Mardagg took possession of him.

'By Sigmar, let there be some pity...' Notker's pleas echoed through the chapel.

The daemon's claws closed around Notker's head. Blood cascaded from the man's neck as the monster pulled. His body started to lift off the ground, then there was a wet, tearing sound, and it flopped to the floor without its head.

The daemon opened its hand and looked at the ghastly trophy it held. Then its malignant gaze swept across the rest of the chapel. Magda thought the fleshless skull smiled at them. The monster crumpled to its knees. The tattered flesh and elongated bones began to bubble and froth. A pink foam erupted from its mouth and chest, from the now empty sockets of its skull. Slimy strings of blood drooled from its giant body, pooling on the floor in a mire of gory scum.

The long arms crumbled, disintegrating into a charnel mash. The chest melted into crimson ooze. The skull sank into the putrid mass, its bones boiling away. Soon all that remained was bloody residue, a few tatters of cloth and the soiled blade of Ottokar Hausler.

'It... it is dead!' Roald exclaimed.

Magda looked away from the corpse of her father and glanced over at the baron. 'No,' she said. 'It simply left Reiner to find itself another host.'

CHAPTER VI

Roald poured himself another glass of brandy. The first had steadied his hand enough that this time only a little of the liquor spilled across the mahogany cabinet. The baron drank it down in a single jolt. At once he felt a fortifying warmth rush through him. Feeling more secure, he turned from the cabinet and looked across the room.

The surviving guests were back in the parlour. No one had any desire to linger in the chapel.

So much for the vaunted protection of Sigmar.

Roald looked across to Hiltrude and Liebgarde. His wife and daughter were sitting together on a couch, each holding the other's hand. The baroness retained a stolid appearance, but she didn't fool Roald. There was just a bit too much detachment in the expression for it to be real. Inside, he knew, she was every bit as rattled as the wide-eyed Liebgarde. A slight bit of positivity to come out of this horror, he thought.

The two duardin were keeping to themselves, leaning

against the far wall of the room. They'd appropriated two decanters from the liquor cabinet and were gradually draining the contents. Even so, there was a sharpness about their eyes as they watched the door leading into the hall. Roald wasn't sure what they thought they'd see. The daemon certainly wasn't going to make much use of the pile of mush it had turned Reiner into. The thing would need a new host to continue its murderous work.

Hartmann and his children were sitting near the fireplace. The younger Senfs were distraught over Sigune's horrible death. They sat close together on two chairs, crying and consoling one another. Their father was standing apart from them. He was trying to keep his eyes focused on the fire, but Roald caught the merchant casting furtive glances at Heimo and Herlinde. When he looked at his children, it wasn't with sympathy. Hartmann had the attitude of a rabbit watching a fox. It wasn't hard to understand the reason for his fear. The rest of them had only a single child for the daemon to possess. Hartmann's chances that he would be the next to be marked for death were double.

The Walkenhorsts and the Hauslers were together, gathered around the divan. The Hauslers were taking the death of Ottokar hard, especially the daughter. Magda sat staring at the floor, unresponsive to the efforts of Inge and Bernger to comfort her. Bruno stood away from the three, one hand on the hilt of his sword. As though he'd be able to do anything to protect them when the time came.

The Krebs and Abarahm were towards the back of the room. Lothar was having a hushed conversation with the aelf while his son stood back and listened. As ever, Saskia had that listless, careless attitude, slouched in a chair with a vapid expression on her pretty face. Roald wasn't sure what concoction the alchemist was administering to his wife, but its potency couldn't be argued. Even the scene in the chapel hadn't been enough to rouse the woman.

Roald took up one of the empty glasses from the cabinet. He dashed it to the floor with a dramatic flourish. The sound of breaking glass had everyone except Saskia looking his way. The baron seized upon their attention.

'Well, now we know that the count's threats are real,' Roald said. 'No room for doubt now. The question is, what are we going to do about it?'

Alrik ran his hand through his beard and shook his head. 'Last idea someone came up with was to hide in the chapel. That didn't work out so well. The daemon was there just waitin'. Like it already knew what was goin' to happen.'

The cogsmith's words had Hartmann recoiling away from the fireplace. 'Can that be true? Does the... thing know what we're going to do before we do it?'

'The daemons of Khorne are not known for their subtly,' Lothar said. The alchemist smiled at Hartmann. 'The... Mardagg is a being that exists only to kill. To harvest death for the Blood God. In such readings as I have made into the subject, there is no suggestion that it has any prophetic abilities. Fate and possibility are more the province of the daemons that serve Tzeentch.'

'Yet it knew we would go to the chapel,' Roald pointed out. 'You can't deny that.'

Lothar conceded the point, but had an explanation. 'When it took possession of Reiner, the daemon also claimed the boy's mind and memories. It knew everything Reiner knew about his father. From that, it could predict that Notker would pray for the protection of Sigmar and seek safety in the chapel.'

'It looked like it knew who was going to strike at it before they did,' Magda said, her voice cracking with emotion. 'It *knew* my father was going to attack it.'

'Coincidence,' Lothar said, but there was uncertainty in his tone. He shook his head. 'No, it was only using Reiner's knowledge to plot its actions.'

'But would the daemon subject itself to the sanctity of such a place?' Hiltrude wondered. Roald took a grim pleasure in the undercurrent of fear behind her words.

'There was no sanctity in the chapel,' Lothar stated. 'If there had been, the daemon could not have long endured there. Yet it must have been hidden in Hagen's sepulchre for hours. No, whatever sanctity had been there was abolished.' He paused and nodded as he connected an idea. 'Yes, by Notker himself. Recall what he said about removing the ancient protections placed in Mhurghast by the Stormcasts? He did not scruple about de-sanctifying even Sigmar's chapel. Reiner must have known what he'd done.'

'At Count Wulfsige's behest,' Bruno cursed.

Roald walked towards Lothar. 'But was Notker aware of *why* he was doing it? Did he know this hellish night was part of the count's plans?' The baron shook his head. 'I think not. No man of Notker's timidity would stick his head into the dragon's mouth like that. Perhaps he agreed as a concession to the count's loss of faith in Sigmar after Hagen's suicide.'

'There can be no question that Notker was unaware of why he was de-sanctifying the castle,' Lothar stated. He looked over at Abarahm. The aelf motioned with his slender fingers for him to continue.

'I have been consulting with Abarahm, asking if his mother had any contact with the count after Hagen's death. His information confirms my worries. It was from Nushala Iliviar that he learned of the…' He hesitated before speaking the fearsome name. 'Mardagg, and how it might be summoned. The count had consulted with her frequently on the subject of daemons. It is no doubt a measure of her arrogance that she believed no human could possibly put such esoteric knowledge to use.'

A ghastly realisation struck Roald. One that made him quiver inside. 'Then it may have been more than conceit that caused her to walk into the courtyard and be shot,' he said. 'She was afraid because she knew what it was the count had called.'

'Certainly more than any of us did.' Lothar turned and looked over at the duardin. 'Notker and Nushala were not the only ones who did work for the count after Hagen's death.'

Bernger let go of Magda's arm and rose from the divan. He pointed an accusing finger at Alrik. 'Those traps in the dungeon. You built them!'

Brond stepped forwards and glowered at Bernger. 'Aye, my father designed and built the traps you saw.' An ugly leer pulled at the duardin's beard. 'More, even. Some you didn't see.'

'The count said he wanted protection for the castle,' Alrik said. 'He was worried about the entrance below Mhurghast.'

Of all that Roald had heard, it was that statement that introduced a ray of hope. He pounced on the comment. 'Then there is a way out through the dungeon. You built the traps – you must know how to get around them! You can show us the way through. You can get all of us out of the castle!'

Alrik's gaze was defiant when he looked at Roald. 'We took an oath when we took the job. An oath of secrecy.'

'You can't be serious!' Hartmann cried. He gestured at the other guests. 'All our lives are in danger! Even yours! You have to get us out!'

The cogsmith remained steadfast. 'Maybe for manlings it is different, but for duardin, an oath is more important than life. Without your honour, you are less than dead.' Alrik grinned at the merchant. 'Besides, I don't think any of us didn't help the count in some way. Notker de-sanctified the castle, the aelf told him about the daemon, I built the traps to close off the dungeon. What was your part?'

All the colour drained out of Hartmann's face. 'I... I did nothing,' he protested as he backed away.

'I believe the cogsmith is right,' Lothar said. 'It must have suited the count's twisted thirst for vengeance that each of us should contribute to our own destruction. A kind of oblivious self-destruction to match the self-destruction of his son.' The alchemist looked carefully at the others, then fixed his attention back on Hartmann. 'When we came here, none of us understood the importance of the work we did for the count. Now... now we do. What was your role, Herr Senf?'

Roald rounded on the alchemist. 'What part did you play, Herr Krebs?'

Lothar's expression grew grave. He laid a hand on Saskia's shoulder and gave her a sad look. 'My wife nearly died when giving birth to Thilo. After that I devised a potion that would ensure such danger would never threaten her again.' He turned and faced the other guests. 'The count learned of the potion somehow and hired me to provide him–'

'Sigmar's Grace!' Inge exclaimed. She stood up and looked in horror at the alchemist. 'All of us. Only one child.'

'Sigune Senf had twins,' Lothar stated, 'and of course there was no need to act where the duardin and aelf were concerned.' He gestured with his sinuous hands. 'For some of you it was enough to simply bribe a servant to add a drop or two in your milk, or your brandy, or your tea. A few of you were a little more difficult... but I managed.'

Hiltrude glared at Lothar. 'You miserable, scheming spider! Poisoning me. Me!'

Roald felt his own temper boiling over. But for Lothar's potion, Hiltrude might have given him sons to carry on his legacy. He gripped the decanter by its neck, ready to smash it across the alchemist's face.

'Before you invest all your hate upon me, perhaps you might ask Baron von Woernhoer what he did for the count,' Lothar stated. 'Or do you deny you did him any favours, your lordship? Maybe with the promise of a legacy when Count Wulfsige died?'

The decanter fell from Roald's fingers and clattered across the floor. It was not the accusation voiced by Lothar that gave him pause, but the look from Hiltrude. He could tell that she knew he'd done something to contribute to the count's insidious plan. He felt all eyes on him, waiting to hear what he would say.

'Why shouldn't I tell you?' Roald scoffed. 'There is nothing shameful in it. The count wanted certain people observed. Kept tabs on.'

'And acted upon if it seemed they might leave Ravensbach,' Hiltrude said. 'That is why you were so insistent on some of your business dealings...'

Roald turned to her. 'Yes! Because I thought by doing so we would gain the confidence of Count Wulfsige. The authority of the von Woernhoers would be magnified by the wealth of the von Koeterbergs. I'd have raised the prestige of your house to a degree that would impress even you.' He walked over to Hiltrude and took her hands in his. 'Everything I have done is for your benefit,' he assured her.

Before Roald could accurately judge the impression he had made on the baroness, Bruno decided to confess the errand he'd performed for the late count. He stepped around the divan so that he could look at Inge and Magda.

'I crippled Ottokar,' Bruno said. The declaration evoked horrified surprise from both women.

'But... but it couldn't...' Inge muttered.

'Ottokar never told you who he fought,' Bruno continued. 'Who it was who cost him his arm. At least, I was responsible.' He lowered his head, unable to hold Inge's gaze. 'For weeks I had heard stories about how Ottokar was mistreating you, abusing you.'

Inge shook her head in disbelief. 'Ottokar never...'

'If that is true, then we can guess where these stories started,' Roald said. 'More of the count's plotting. Ottokar Hausler was the most feared blade in Ravensbach. Not a man you want to invite to a murder party.'

Bruno nodded at the baron. 'I learned afterwards that the stories were untrue. I saw for myself what kind of man Ottokar was after he was crippled. Those first days, when Inge stayed by his side. The brute who had been described to me could never have warranted such devotion.'

Magda stood and glared at Bruno. 'Never mind why. What did you do to my father?'

'I thought your mother was in distress. No, there was no longer anything between us, but that did not mean I stopped caring about what happened to her.' Again Bruno lowered his head in shame. 'I knew I would lose if I crossed swords with Ottokar. At the same time I felt compelled to stop him. So I hired Anton Gerver to challenge him. Anton was not a better swordsman, but he was a vicious scoundrel without scruples. When he duelled with Ottokar, he had a pistol hidden under his cloak. Your father was quick enough to turn when Anton fired, so the shot hit him in the arm. Ottokar was able to kill Anton before collapsing in the street from his wound.'

Bernger stood beside Bruno, shock on his face. 'You speak as though you saw it happen.'

'That is because I did,' Bruno replied. 'I watched the duel, and afterwards I stepped out to finish what Anton started. But as I stared down at Ottokar, sprawled helpless in the street, I did not have the stomach to strike him. I chose my assassin because he was without any sense of honour. I had too much.'

'So that is why he said that the man who hired his attacker no longer had any interest,' Magda snarled. Her eyes blazed with a vengeful light. Roald thought for a moment she was going to fly at Bruno, but Inge coaxed her back to the divan.

'That would bring us back to Hartmann,' Roald said as he walked towards the fireplace. He fixed the fat merchant with an expectant stare. 'What skeleton do you have rattling around in your cellar?'

Hartmann balked at the demand. He licked his lips anxiously, his eyes darting from side to side like a cornered beast's. 'I... I had business... dealings with Count Wulfsige. The same... the same as you, your lordship.'

'Don't claim innocence,' Roald said. 'One look at you is enough to tell anyone you are as guilty as the rest of us.' He thrust his finger against Hartmann's chest and prodded the merchant backwards until he was up against the wall. 'You know exactly what you did and how it helped create this night of horror. What was it?'

'Okay... okay,' Hartmann sobbed, sweat peppering his brow. 'I put him in contact with a tradesman, one Gustav Krause. Count Wulfsige was looking for a specific item, something too exotic for me to handle. Something Gustav, with his wide associations, might be able to find.'

Roald stepped away, disgust on his face. 'The dagger. That weird dagger the count used to cut his own throat. He needed it to call the daemon... and you told him how to find it.'

'But I didn't know,' Hartmann protested. 'I didn't know why he wanted it. By Sigmar, I swear I didn't know!'

'Ignorance,' Lothar grumbled. 'That will be small consolation when the daemon comes to take your life.'

'All of your lives are already forfeit.'

The cold, commanding voice came from the hallway. Roald and the other guests turned to see a man walk into the parlour. Someone who had not been present at the dinner and who was not one of the castle servants. He was a tall man garbed in a long black cloak. The broad-brimmed hat he wore cast his face in shadow, but there was no mistaking the large medal pinned to the breast of his dark tunic. The gold badge was cast in the shape of a twin-tailed comet, a symbol sacred to Sigmar. It was the emblem of the God-King's most feared mortal servants. The Order of Azyr.

The witch hunters.

Fear rippled through the guests when they saw the black-clad witch hunter standing in the doorway, but Magda's reaction was much different. An excitement raced through her, momentarily subduing her despair over Ottokar and her fury towards Bruno. All she could think of was the desperate hope she had nurtured since crying out to the men in the courtyard.

Klueger was here!

The witch hunter whipped away his hat as he entered the parlour. Klueger's eyes were ice-blue, often so cold that they seemed reptilian to Magda. Now they had a different sort of intensity. Concern shone in his gaze when he looked at her, a concern so powerful that it bordered upon madness. He took one step towards her, then the expression on his hawkish features became grave.

'What do you mean, all our lives are forfeit?' Roald cried out.

Klueger turned to the baron. His glacial eyes stared straight into the nobleman's. 'Everyone in this castle has been condemned by Grand Lector Sieghard,' he announced. 'The threat of the daemon is too great. He will not allow anyone to leave here alive.' He bowed to Roald. 'That includes your lordship.'

Roald's face turned crimson. He held the hand that had been injured towards Klueger. 'Sieghard is simply trying to cover for himself. He knows he has overstepped his authority. I will not stand for this outrage!' He motioned to Hiltrude. 'The Baroness von Woernhoer has powerful connections–'

'None of whom wish to be possessed by a daemon... or killed by one,' Klueger replied acidly. 'The danger here is too great. Nobody is going to help you.'

'Except you,' Magda said. Even as she spoke, she wondered if it was out of hope or from doubt. She hurried over to Klueger's side. 'You came to help. That is why you were allowed through the quarantine.'

Klueger took her hand in his, the leather of his glove tightening around her fingers. 'I came here because I couldn't do otherwise. I don't know what I can do, but I know I have to do something.'

'A fine thing for you to say,' Bernger growled. 'You aren't being targeted by the count's revenge.'

Klueger explained the threat that hung over his head. 'I won't be allowed back through the quarantine,' he stated. 'My passage through the cordon was one way only. It's fortunate for you that I have a personal interest in this affair.'

'Then you are trapped here with the rest of us?' Magda asked, afraid to accept that dire prospect, feeling guilty that she had drawn him into their plight.

'I regret nothing,' Klueger assured her. 'And it may be that I can find a way to break the curse.' He looked across at the others. 'That is your only chance. If I can convince the grand lector that the daemon is gone, he may allow you to leave. But time is short.'

Roald shook his head. 'Tell Sieghard it is gone then! Your neck is in the noose now too!'

'I won't put everyone in Ravensbach in jeopardy,' Klueger

said. He squeezed Magda's hand. 'Not even with all I stand to lose. Besides, your lordship, if I fail to convince the grand lector, he will go ahead with his plan to put everything inside Mhurghast to the torch.'

Shock rippled through the room. Magda felt the hope inside her flicker and die. The daemon, the ghastly traps in the dungeon, and now this, the promise of being burned alive by the grand lector's mob.

'How can you stop that from happening?' she asked.

Klueger released her hand and walked to the centre of the parlour. 'First you will tell me everything that has happened. Every detail is important. Once I know what has transpired here, then maybe I will know what action to take.'

No secrets were kept from Klueger. The doom hanging over them removed even Hartmann's reticence. Magda felt anger flare up inside her when she listened to Bruno explain about crippling her father for the second time. When everyone was finished, Klueger looked at Inge.

'It's not hard to guess the part you played in helping the count plan his vengeance,' he said.

Inge stared at him in bewilderment. 'But I hadn't seen Count Wulfsige since...'

'Since Hagen died,' Klueger finished for her. 'That, for the count, was enough. To him, you were the instigator of all this. Your mere existence gave him the determination to persist, no matter what foulness was demanded of him to achieve his revenge.'

'What do the count's motivations matter?' Lothar asked. 'What is needed is a way to thwart this daemon. Has anything we've told you suggested a way to defeat it?'

Klueger turned to the alchemist. 'I will have to see for myself the evidence the daemon left behind. Once I have seen that, I will have a better idea of its power.'

'That would mean goin' back to the chapel,' Alrik said.

Magda knew what Klueger would need. 'I will show you the way,' she said.

'We don't know if there is still danger,' Bernger objected.

The witch hunter had an answer for him. 'Where the daemon has already been isn't the place of danger. It's where the fiend will go next. And in whom. Right now it's gathering its strength to seize a new host. When it's ready, one of you in this room will feel its evil consuming you.'

Magda repressed a shudder at the thought of ending up like Reiner. More, the daemon would use her to kill her mother. It was a hideous doom, the kind of horror only a monster would conceive. Then her eyes strayed to Bruno and she felt her own lust for revenge blazing inside her.

'I'll show you the way,' she said. Magda's expression was resolute as she led Klueger from the room. 'There's something I left in the chapel that I want to get.'

For a time, as Magda guided Klueger through the dark halls, they could still hear the murmur of conversation emanating from the parlour. It was only when they were too far to hear the guests that Klueger spoke.

'Whatever happens, I'll get you out of here,' he said.

Magda could see the desperation on his visage. It was unlike the cold confidence she was accustomed to. Klueger wielded considerable authority as a witch hunter, and was the final arbiter of life and death for those who fell within his purview. He had to be certain and steadfast in his convictions. The slightest doubt would bring his judgement into question, and that was something the Order of Azyr could not afford.

Yet here he was, frightened and uncertain. Vulnerable. All because, Magda realised, he was afraid. Not for himself, but for her.

'There's more than just me to think about,' Magda reminded him. 'You have obligations.'

'I will not betray them,' Klueger vowed. 'There'll be no need to. In times of darkness it's faith in Sigmar that sustains us. Faith in the justness of His power and His dominion.'

Instead of being assured by Klueger's words, Magda felt a chill run through her. She was thinking of the chapel. Notker might have lost his faith, but Sigune had been devout in her beliefs. The daemon had killed her just the same.

The two walked on in silence, their footsteps echoing through the iron halls. Magda could feel the enormous age of Mhurghast pressing in on her. All the stories she'd heard about it while growing up came back to her again. The castle was ancient beyond reckoning, a relic from another time. It had served as a bastion of civilisation, a fortress from which the champions of order defended the land from the hordes of Chaos. Before that, however, it had been the citadel of the enemy, a place of evil and horror. That sinister legacy persisted, soaked into the very foundations. Magda could feel it rising up, rallying to the nightmare conjured by Count Wulfsige's hate.

'This is the chapel,' she said as their path drew them to the iron gate. Her step faltered as they approached.

Klueger laid his hand on her shoulder. 'There's no need for you to enter,' he said.

Magda looked past him, her eyes focused upon the horrible memories. 'No, I have to do this.'

The witch hunter held her close. 'I'm sorry about Ottokar. He was a good man. He died the way a warrior should die. Fighting to protect those he loves.' Klueger stared into Magda's eyes. 'Every breath, every heartbeat, with it you pay respect to his sacrifice. Your father bought you the rest of your life when he fought the daemon.'

Magda wanted to accept Klueger's consoling words, but they fell hollow in her ears. Ottokar had thought he could save them when he attacked the daemon, but the thought was different from the deed. His death had been pointless. The daemon endured. Magda didn't need to be told that by some expert of the occult. She could feel it, sense it scratching at the edge of reality like a wolf pawing at a locked door.

The lock was weakening. Soon the door would open.

'Come on,' Magda said. She drew away from Klueger and stepped towards the gate. The witch hunter drew the sword he carried, a slender blade fashioned from silvery metal. Klueger had told her that it had been fashioned in Azyrheim from sigmarite, the fabulous metal used by the mighty Stormcast Eternals. It could harm creatures otherwise inured to physical injury. Things like daemons.

'Keep behind me,' Klueger said as he stepped past Magda and cautiously entered the chapel. He emphasised his meaning by nodding at the falchion she'd brought with her from the parlour. 'Your blade is merely steel.' He reached to the holster on his hip and handed her the gold-handled pistol he carried. 'If there's something here, use this. The bullets are blessed by the grand lector. The charge will hold for six shots. Just aim, squeeze the trigger and pray to Sigmar.'

'I'd be more use with the sword,' Magda reminded him. She was unfamiliar with pistols, but almost from the cradle she'd learned how to handle a blade.

The witch hunter strode forwards, his gaze sweeping across the dusty pews. 'If there's something here, I know how I'll react to its presence.' He turned, a pained look on his face. 'I mean I have been trained…'

Magda just nodded in reply. Klueger did not have to say anything else. There was the threat that the daemon might possess her, just as it might possess any of the children. The witch hunter was willing to risk the pistol – he had a second on his belt – but not his sigmarite sword. Magda did not press him further. She didn't want to know if, should she be possessed, Klueger would be able to strike her down.

The guests had done nothing to cover the gory scene around the altar. The bodies lay strewn about the bloody pulp that had once been Reiner. Magda stifled a sob when she saw the twisted remains of Ottokar's silver arm. Tears welled up in her eyes when she saw her father's corpse. It was more than a look of horror that was frozen on his face – an expression of agonising despair. In his last moments, he'd tried to save her. When death took him, it came with the knowledge that he'd failed.

This time Klueger was oblivious to Magda's distress. Training and instinct took over, and the witch hunter prowled about the carnage like a gryph-hound. He examined the bodies, the shattered altar. He stood beside the broken sepulchre and studied what was inside. Then, with a visible repugnance, he knelt beside the fleshy mash that had been the daemon's host body. He drew a long silvery pin from a pocket and began to prod the remains.

'I hoped... I prayed that your stories were wrong,' Klueger said. 'I wanted to believe you were all mistaken, that the count had conjured some lesser fiend to haunt you.'

Magda approached the altar. Her eyes kept straying back to Ottokar's body. 'Whatever he conjured, it has to be killed.'

Klueger stood. His face was desolate. 'A daemon can't be killed, because it's not really alive. It can only be vanquished, sent back to the cursed Realm of Chaos.' His voice dropped to a grave whisper. 'Magda, this thing is more powerful than anything I have seen. Every speck of Reiner's flesh has been corrupted, befouled with the daemon's essence. Only a manifestation of obscene power could do such a thing.' A shudder passed through him as he told her the bitter truth he'd been forced to accept. 'Magda, I don't know if I *can* stop this thing.'

Magda felt her insides turn cold. The bold, confident witch hunter was now unsure of himself. To hear a man of sincere faith express doubt was somehow more horrible than the fear and despair of all the others.

Magda stared at the fleshy pulp. She reached down and withdrew the blade that was partially buried in the gore. Ottokar's sword. Her father's sword. It was why she'd come back to the chapel. She intended to avenge her father.

'Maybe we can't stop the daemon,' she said, 'but that doesn't mean it takes us without a fight.'

Bernger stood with the others as they tried to interrogate the duardin. After the witch hunter left, Hartmann had brought up the idea that they shouldn't waste time trying to fight the daemon. They should get out of the castle. Abarahm supported the idea. The stronger the daemon, the harder it was for the fiend to maintain itself away from the Realm of Chaos. The ancient sorceries that had once dominated Mhurghast might allow it to manifest in the castle, but outside would be different. Or so it was hoped. Of one thing there was certainty. Remaining inside the castle was waiting for certain death.

'An oath is an oath,' Alrik snarled. He held the broken leg of a chair in his hands and waved it menacingly at his interrogators. 'I'd sooner die than be an oathbreaker.'

'Be sensible,' Abarahm advised. 'It is not just your life in jeopardy, but that of your son. Would you sacrifice him because of a promise made to a dead man? A dead man who planned for both of you to die?'

Alrik glanced over at his son, then sneered at the aelf. 'If I broke my oath, the shame of it would pass on to Brond, and to his children and their children's children.'

'Don't you feel any responsibility for those people who died in your traps?' Bernger demanded. 'I saw them. Impaled on spikes. Cooked alive on those red-hot walls.'

The cogsmith shrugged. 'I only did what I was paid to do.'

Hiltrude began removing her jewellery. 'If it is a question of money, I will pay you to show us how to get past–'

'It isn't the money,' Brond said. 'It's our oath. We cannot break it.'

Bernger gestured to Bruno. 'I would do anything for my father,' he said. 'What about you? You can save your father by telling us how to get past the traps.'

'Don't let them turn your head,' Alrik warned Brond. 'I'll not have an oathbreaker for a son. Tell them anything and you are no longer of my blood.'

'This is idiotic!' Roald shouted. He stormed towards the duardin. 'You would let all of us die for some bombastic notion of honour!' He glanced around at the other guests. 'There are only two of them. I say we rush them and make them tell.' He pointed at Alrik. 'Maybe after I use a hot poker to trim that beard, you'll feel more like talking.'

Howling with outrage, Brond rushed Roald. The nobleman retreated before the duardin's charge. He fell over the divan and lay sprawled on the floor. Brond stood over him and raised his mattock for a downward swing.

Bruno and Bernger hurried to catch hold of the duardin while Roald scrambled away. Brond proved surprisingly strong. He threw them off and glared at the baron's defenders.

'His eyes! By Sigmar, look at his eyes!' Bruno cried as he backed away.

Bernger stared in horror at Brond. The duardin's eyes were completely red. A trickle of blood dripped from the corner of each like crimson tears.

Brond's rage faltered. Haltingly, he lifted a hand to his

face and touched the blood falling down his cheeks. A wail of terror rose from him when he saw the crimson patina on his fingers. He cast aside his mattock and ran out into the hallway.

'Brond!' Alrik shouted. He started to chase after his son, but only managed a few steps before guests were swarming over him. Heimo threw a chair in the cogsmith's path, sending him to the floor. Thilo and Abarahm pounced on the sprawled duardin, pinning him down while Lothar poured a strange liquid onto a blanket. Before Alrik could free himself, the alchemist threw the damp blanket over his head. Almost instantly the cogsmith's efforts to escape lessened. Soon he was completely insensible.

'We can't let the other one go,' Roald shouted in panic. 'The daemon's inside him. It'll come back.'

'I'll get him,' Bernger said. Only after the words left his mouth and he was dashing out into the hallway did it occur to him that he had no idea what he would do even if he caught up to Brond. What could he possibly do with someone who at any moment might turn into a daemon and rend his flesh as it had those it butchered in the chapel?

Bernger turned when he heard footsteps pounding after him. His father came dashing down the hallway, his sword drawn. There was an intense severity in his expression.

'If we catch up to him, we kill him,' Bruno told his son, shocking him with the brutality of his words. 'It might be the only way. Kill the host while he's still mortal enough to be killed. Brond's already as good as dead anyway. If we act fast, maybe we can keep him from killing his own father.'

Bernger was still aghast at the plan. 'It's monstrous.'

Bruno agreed. 'Sometimes what needs to be done isn't what we'd like it to be.'

The two men could hear Brond's steps far ahead of them.

Terror had lent the duardin a shocking fleetness. Or perhaps it was the daemon possessing him that made him so quick. Bernger wondered if it might already be too late to stop the fiend.

'He's headed for the courtyard,' Bruno suddenly realised as they started into the long corridor that led to the castle entrance.

Bernger appreciated what motivated Brond. 'He has the same idea we do. He thinks if he can die quick enough he can dislodge the daemon and keep it from going after his father.'

'Prey without a hunter,' Bruno muttered. 'Hunter without prey.'

Bernger thought of something else. 'Grand Lector Sieghard! What'll he think if he sees Brond like this?'

'He might be moved to storm the castle and burn everything – everyone – inside!'

Bernger redoubled his pace, coaxing every last speck of speed he could from his body. He had to catch the duardin now. He couldn't let the men in the courtyard see him.

'Bernger!' Bruno yelled. 'He's turned away. He isn't running for the courtyard any more!' He pointed to a side passage. He waited only long enough to be sure his son knew where he was going before he ducked into the corridor.

Bernger found there was something familiar about the passage. After the second turn he knew what it was. This was the way Goswin and the servants had gone to reach the trophy room.

'He's headed for the dungeons!' Bernger shouted to Bruno.

Bruno let his pace slacken. 'Then we're too late.'

'We can catch him,' Bernger assured his father.

'Why did he turn back from the courtyard? I don't think it was because he was afraid of upsetting Sieghard.'

'He may have. He may have decided to use the traps to…'

Bruno shook his head. 'We'll see,' he said, but there was no confidence in his voice.

The two men reached the trophy room without catching sight of Brond. Bernger thought he heard hurried footsteps echoing from the hidden passage. He raced over to the secret door and peered into the dark opening. He could detect the faint noise of someone moving below.

'He's here!' Bernger called before darting into the stairway. Bruno hurried after him.

Bernger emerged from the passage just in time to see Brond finish crossing the first of the trapped corridors. 'We have him now!' He started for the dungeon, but his father caught hold of him and pulled him back.

'It's too late,' Bruno said.

'I know how to cross the first two rooms. I saw Goswin do it.'

Bruno gestured to the corridor where one wrong step would see a trespasser impaled on the spikes. 'Brond could have killed himself right here. He didn't. That means he didn't come here to destroy himself. He came to hide somewhere we can't follow. Just like Reiner, the daemon needs time to fully claim its host.'

'Then Baron von Woernhoer is right,' Bernger said. 'We have to make Alrik tell us the secrets of the dungeon.'

Bruno nodded. 'Maybe he'll listen now. Maybe now that he sees what has happened to his son, he'll see everything else in a new light.'

There was a sombre note in Bruno's tone that echoed through the cellar. To Bernger it had all the qualities of a portent of doom.

CHAPTER VII

Roald watched the iron heating in the fire. He wasn't a squeamish man, but he did consider such things to be dirty and sordid. The kind of work he paid people to do for him, not perform on his own. He sent a contemptuous glance at Lothar. Of course the alchemist would have a few of his vile potions among his effects, such as the one that had subdued Alrik, but he didn't happen to have any of the ingredients for the mixture he claimed could compel anyone to answer questions put to them.

'Be sensible, damn you!' Roald spun around and glared at the duardin. Alrik was bound hand and foot, sitting in the same seat Goswin had sat in hours ago. There was no fear in the cogsmith's gaze, only an insolent defiance that to the baron felt like a personal affront.

'It is foolish of you to stay quiet,' Hiltrude said, her tone more diplomatic than Roald's. She was always like that, always adopting a manner that would make her appear more controlled and commanding than her husband. 'Brond has become the daemon's new host. That means you are its next victim. Time is short for all of us, but even more so for you.'

Hartmann dropped to his knees beside Alrik. 'You've got to tell us how to get past the traps,' he implored. 'None of us are poor. We'll pay you handsomely–'

'Stop grovelling,' Roald snarled. 'You won't make an impression on him that way. He's already made it clear he doesn't care about money.' He withdrew the iron from the fire. The faint glow around its pronged tip wasn't to his satisfaction, so he thrust it back into the flames.

Abarahm paced behind Alrik's chair, the aelf's clothing rippling with an uncanny motion, as though it were woven from oceanic waves. 'The duardin are renowned for their stubbornness,' he said. 'It will be useless to threaten him. Even more to torture him.'

'I must agree,' Thilo said. He walked towards Roald. 'If we lower ourselves to this kind of thing... what does that make us?'

Roald's eyes were cold when he answered. 'Alive. And that is all that matters right now.' He glanced over at Hiltrude, but the baroness had nothing to add. Liebgarde was sitting at the far end of the room, putting as much distance between herself and Alrik as she could. She was always timid, Roald reflected. That was Hiltrude's fault, for pampering her too much.

'There is the chance the witch hunter could find a way to stop the daemon,' Lothar suggested. 'Men in that profession are not without their own abilities.'

'The only person here Klueger cares about saving is that girl,' Roald said. He turned towards Inge. 'Is that not so, Frau Hausler? If not for your daughter, would that man have dared pass through Sieghard's quarantine?'

Inge met the baron's sharp gaze. 'I often advised her against associating with that man. They're a fearsome breed. I wanted better things for her, a loftier future. But right now I thank Sigmar for the bond between them. Klueger will do everything he can to protect Magda.' She looked across the room at the rest of the guests. 'Magda is the only one I care about.' She pointed at Alrik. 'This barbarous farce makes me wonder if any of you even deserve to live.'

Roald smiled at the retort. 'There you have it. From the mother's own mouth. All the witch hunter cares about is saving that girl.' He moved back towards the chair and loomed over Alrik. 'You'll talk. I promise you. I'll singe that beard down to stubble. Brand your cheeks down to the jawbone if I have to. You'll talk. Save yourself a lot of pain and just tell us now.'

Alrik merely stared back at Roald. Not with anger, or fear, but with that same fatalistic insolence. Roald spun around and snatched the iron from the fire. He tested its heat on the rug, searing a long stripe across it. He gestured with its glowing tip at the cogsmith's face.

'This against that,' Roald warned. He fought to keep his tone measured, to keep an edge of panic from his voice. For the first time it had occurred to him that even under torture Alrik might stay silent. 'Last chance. How do we get through the traps in the dungeon?'

'Do it already,' Hartmann hissed. The merchant's eyes were frantic, his face glistening with sweat. 'Make him tell us how to get away! Force it out of him!'

Roald hesitated. He looked aside to Hiltrude. He caught the slight nod she gave him. At least he wouldn't have to worry about her disapproval later. He firmed his grip on the poker and stepped towards the chair. The hot iron slashed down, raking across Alrik's cheek. The stink of burnt hair rose from the duardin. Just like the rug, a blackened stripe ran through the cogsmith's beard.

Roald took a step back when Alrik didn't cry out. He simply stared at the baron with the same defiant indifference. Roald was prepared for rage or terror, but not this sort of resignation. How could he torture someone who didn't even care about what was happening to him?

'Make him talk!' Hartmann cried. 'He has to talk!'

Roald raised the iron to strike again. Before he could, the sound of someone running in the corridor outside brought him up short. Except for the captive Alrik, everyone turned towards the doorway, their hands tightening around whatever weapon they'd found for themselves. Hartmann scrambled back and uttered a sob of horror.

Their dread proved unfounded when Bernger came into the parlour. He was flushed from his recent exertions and it took him several moments to recover his breath so that he could speak.

'We didn't catch Brond,' Bernger finally reported. 'It looked like he was headed towards the courtyard. That he might use Sieghard's men to kill himself before the daemon could take complete control.'

Roald clenched his fist in frustration. Now it was going to be even harder to get Alrik to talk. However, the germ of an idea took shape in his mind. An idea that horrified even him.

'You said it *looked* like he was headed for the courtyard?' Hiltrude prompted Bernger.

Bernger shook his head. 'He turned. We followed him down into the dungeon. We thought maybe he was going to use the traps to... stop the daemon. But we followed as far as the first room, and there was no sign of his body. We could hear someone moving further on. Past where I lost sight of Goswin.'

'It is the daemon,' Lothar declared. 'It knows everything Brond knows, which would include how the traps work and how to get past them. It has used that to hide itself while it completes its transformation.' The alchemist shuddered. 'When next we see him, he will be in the same state that Reiner was.'

Inge slumped in her chair, seeming to wilt into the seat. 'When we see him, he'll be coming to kill his father.' Roald understood her terror. None of them were thinking about the duardin. They were all thinking that the same horrible doom threatened all of them.

'Right now the daemon will still be weak,' Lothar said. 'It is caught between two spheres, two planes of reality. It needs time to pour enough of its essence into Brond to completely manifest. It hides because during this process it is vulnerable.'

Abarahm was not so certain as the alchemist. 'It is reckless to speak in absolutes when dealing with Chaos. There are certain rites that open the door for daemons, but once that door has been opened there is no way to be certain how wide the opening is. The transference is not entirely predictable. The daemon might need hours to consume its host in one manifestation – in another the process might take only a few heartbeats.'

'Do you know that, or is it mere supposition?' Roald asked. 'Is there a chance to strike this thing or contain it before… before it does what it was summoned to do?' He looked over at Bernger. 'How certain are you that Brond is under the control of this thing already?'

'I only know that Brond has fled into the dungeons,' Bernger said. 'My father's down there now, waiting to give warning if he sees him… or it… come back.'

'We have a chance,' Lothar insisted. 'If we can kill Brond while the daemon has yet to fully possess him, we might be able to break the chain.'

Roald scowled at Lothar. 'How will we reach Brond? He's safe behind all the traps he and his father built. Unless Alrik tells us…'

'I'll tell none of you anything,' Alrik said, suddenly breaking his silence. 'But I can show you. Cut me loose and I'll show you how to get past the traps.'

Roald gazed down at the cogsmith. He was shocked to see tears on Alrik's face. He had started to think the duardin was as tough as the iron and steel he worked. 'Why?' he asked.

Alrik didn't look up at the baron. 'Because we're talking about my son. If there's a chance to... to kill him... before the daemon takes hold. I'd see his spirit join our ancestors, not be destroyed by this monster. Let me be damned as an oathbreaker – I accept that shame if it lets me redeem Brond.'

Roald nodded as he considered the offer. He wasn't able to gauge duardin as easily as he could humans when it came to duplicity, but he thought Alrik was genuine. 'All right,' he decided. 'Hartmann, free his legs. His arms stay tied until we reach the dungeon.'

While Hartmann worked at untying Alrik's legs, Roald stepped back and replaced the iron in its stand by the fireplace. He was just as happy to have an end to such sordid work.

'We aren't all going down there?' Inge asked. 'Someone has to stay here and tell Magda where we've gone.'

'It would be unwise to put everyone in jeopardy,' Lothar said. He nodded to Abarahm. 'If the daemon has already taken hold of its host, we would be putting all our lives in danger to no good purpose.'

Roald thought about that. There was both wisdom and opportunity in what the alchemist said. 'Since it is my decision, I will go.' He looked over at Hartmann as the merchant helped Alrik to his feet. 'You will go with me, Herr Senf.' The choice was obviously not to his liking.

'I'm going with you,' Bernger stated. 'My father's down there.'

'With the cogsmith that makes four. Five with Bruno,' Roald said. His expression turned grave. 'More than enough lives to gamble on this venture.' He looked at Hiltrude, then turned and swept his gaze across the other guests. 'The rest of you stay here and wait for the witch hunter.'

Roald motioned for Bernger and Hartmann to lead Alrik from the room. He was anxious to be gone now. He didn't trust himself to be in the same room as Liebgarde.

Not with the ghastly plan that was taking shape in the baron's mind.

Only when they reached the cellar and he saw Bruno standing watch outside the dungeon did Bernger feel even somewhat at ease. He'd been too focused on reaching the parlour and getting the secret of the traps from Alrik to think of anything else when he'd left his father. On the way back it was a different matter. He was wracked with guilt for leaving Bruno and afraid of what they might find when they returned.

'Has anything happened?' Bernger asked as he emerged from the secret passage.

Bruno kept his eyes on the dungeon. 'Not so much as a sound. Did the cogsmith say anything?'

Bernger stepped aside so that Hartmann could help Alrik into the cellar. 'He wouldn't tell us, but he did agree to show us.'

Bruno turned around and stared into the duardin's eyes. His expression darkened. 'I'm sorry we couldn't catch your son,' he said.

Alrik shook his head. 'My son's dead already. It's his spirit I'm worried about now. If I can stop the daemon, maybe Brond's spirit can join our ancestors.'

Baron von Woernhoer entered the cellar after the rest of them. Roald frowned at the duardin's words. 'We are at something of an impasse, Herr Walkenhorst. The cogsmith won't betray his oath by word, only through deed. He says he will show us how to get past the traps, but he won't tell us how they work.'

'So someone has to go with him to see how they work,' Bruno said. 'Then he can come back and let everyone know.'

'Oaths are a strange thing to duardin,' Hartmann muttered. 'You can cheat them blind in a deal, so long as you don't betray a single word of your agreement.' The merchant smiled nervously at Alrik. 'Of course, the reverse is true too. Kharadron are quite good at hiding swindles in their oaths.'

Alrik spat on the floor and held his bound arms towards Hartmann. 'I'll need the rest of the ropes undone if I'm to go further.'

'Untie him,' Roald declared. When Hartmann hesitated, Bernger came around and picked at the knotted ropes.

'Understand,' Alrik cautioned, 'I'm only interested in destroying the daemon. You can follow. You can watch. But if you make a mistake, it's no concern of mine.'

Bernger dropped the ropes on the floor and stared at the freed duardin. 'That'd be stupid,' he said. 'I've seen two of your traps in action. It seems to me if someone following you makes a mistake, that'll be the end for everyone. You'd better tell us what to do to get past them.'

Alrik looked uneasy as he considered the point. 'Each secret I betray cuts away at the oath I swore to Count Wulfsige. It comes hard, even now, to accept that shame.'

'You waste time,' Roald reminded him. 'We don't know how long it will be before your son becomes like Reiner.'

'Lead the way,' Bruno told the cogsmith. 'I'll follow you. If we find Brond, maybe I can help.'

'*We* can help,' Bernger corrected him. This time he wasn't going to leave his father no matter what he was told. Bruno must have seen the determination on his face. Whatever protest he might have made went unspoken.

'I will stay here with Hartmann,' Roald said. 'If anything happens, at least we will be able to get word back to the others.' The merchant giggled in relief.

Bernger retrieved one of the torches from the wall. He held it towards the trapped room ahead of them. 'I've seen how this one works. There are certain tiles that are slightly raised. Step on one of them and a spiked ceiling springs down.'

'You'll find the others even more interestin',' Alrik said. 'At least, if any of us live to see them.'

The duardin's sinister words were echoing in Bernger's ears as they headed out across the trapped corridor. The task ahead of them was madness itself. Crossing an unknown succession of rooms, each with some fiendish instrument of death waiting within and their guide resentful of each secret he was forced to divulge. Ahead of them, somewhere in the dreadful maze, was a possessed duardin who even now might be changing into an unstoppable daemon.

'I think he'll be helpful until we find Brond,' Bruno whispered to Bernger. 'After that, watch out. He might decide he can keep his oath if he lures us into a trap.'

A chill slithered down Bernger's spine. 'Dead men tell no tales,' he said.

'Something like that,' Bruno agreed. 'If he does something, be ready to move fast.'

Bernger couldn't help but look up at the ceiling as they crossed to the little landing at the far side of the room. Up above them were the servants who had fallen foul of the spikes. He stared at the cogsmith's back and wondered about the mind that could imagine such ghastly mechanisms.

Heat impressed itself upon Bernger when they turned the corner and saw the next room, the narrow hall with the heated walls to either side and the strange copper floor. The servants who had died here were only blackened lumps on the walls now, only vaguely identifiable as anything human.

Alrik turned to the two men. 'The floor here is too thin to support any weight. Try to run across it and it will warp under your feet and toss you against the walls. That happens and you're cooked. Runes of fire.' He nodded to the symbols cut into the walls.

'I saw Goswin get across,' Bernger said. 'He was crawling on hands and knees, but he made it.'

'There is only one part that is safe,' the cogsmith said. He pointed at the floor. 'A beam that runs right down the middle. Stay on it and you won't lose your balance.'

'And the safest way to do that is to crawl,' Bruno concluded.

Bernger dropped down at the edge of the solid landing and laid his hand on the copper floor. The sides were as thin as Alrik said, but a span as wide as his hand was solid. 'I'll start across,' Bernger said. 'Then you can send Alrik.' He was away before either of them could object.

Crawling across the hall was a hellish experience. After only a few feet, Bernger's body was drenched in sweat. The heat from the walls was nearly overwhelming. Each breath he drew felt like sucking on fire. The smell of cooked flesh filled his nose, and he could feel charred flakes under his hands as he crossed close to where the servants had died. His mind trembled at the image of people trying to race across only to lose their balance and be pitched headlong into the red-hot walls.

At last Bernger reached the landing where he had last seen Goswin. When he pulled himself up, he waved back at Bruno. His father started Alrik across. The cogsmith might have designed the trap, but he crossed with the same tedious crawl Bernger had used. Somehow, watching the duardin creep along was even more unsettling than his own crossing. Bernger dreaded watching Bruno when his turn came.

Finally all three of them were safe on the other side. Alrik held a finger to his lips, then started to remove his boots. Bernger and Bruno followed his example, pulling off their shoes. When all of them were unshod, the duardin motioned them forwards.

Bernger stifled a gasp when he saw what had befallen Goswin. The major-domo's body was lying a few feet inside another narrow corridor. This one was much longer and had iron walls much like the rest of the castle's. Try as he might, Bernger could find no explanation for the ghastly state Goswin was in. The man had been cut in half.

Alrik looked at each of them and again motioned for silence. The cogsmith didn't step into the hall, but rather slid his bare foot onto the floor. He repeated this and silently shuffled his way towards the landing at the other side. Bernger and Bruno followed, copying the duardin's curious progress. It was faster going than crawling across the other hallway, but at the same time far more terrible, not knowing where the instrument of death was hidden.

Alrik stopped when he reached the landing. Bernger felt sick when he saw the cogsmith glance back at them. It would be very easy for him to set the trap in motion while they were both under its threat. Fortunately he was more concerned with putting his boots back on.

'You can gab all you'd like now,' Alrik said when the two men joined him.

'What's in there?' Bruno demanded. 'What killed Goswin?'

The cogsmith chuckled grimly. 'It's enough to know how to get past it.'

'No sound in that room,' Bernger said. He pointed at his bare feet. 'Not even so much as a footfall.'

'Anything louder than a heartbeat would be enough,' Alrik said. 'You'll have a hard time gettin' that gutless Hartmann through there.' The duardin seemed oblivious to the irony in the remark.

'What now?' Bernger asked.

Alrik's face was stern. 'I'm goin' ahead to look for Brond. If you're followin' me, you'd better get your shoes back on.'

'Now hold up!' Bruno called as the duardin circled the corner.

Bernger darted after Alrik, but not so recklessly as to follow him farther than the landing. He stayed on the little patch of safe ground and hurried to fasten the buckles on his shoes. He could see that the room ahead was wide but not so long as the others had been. There was a strange sheen to the floor, a kind of gloss that reflected the torchlight. The ground looked firm enough as the cogsmith crossed it.

'So that's how he's going to play it,' Bruno said as he joined Bernger. 'Show us how to get past the traps but not tell us what they are.'

Bernger had his shoes back on and stepped out onto the floor. 'If we follow exactly behind him...' His words failed when he saw the change in Bruno's face. His expression had changed from irritation to a look of terror. Bernger noticed the charnel reek that drifted through the dungeon. The same gory stench that had surrounded the daemon's earlier manifestation. The sound of raw, wet footfalls echoed in his ears.

Bernger turned and looked across towards the other side of the room. Instantly he felt his blood turn cold. Standing on the opposite landing was the bloody, skeletal daemon. It had completed its domination of Brond's body and moulded his flesh into this horrifying aspect. The Mardagg made no sound as it tilted its skull-like head, but there was a ravenous fire in its sunken eyes.

'Back! Get back! Through the last room!' Alrik scrambled towards them. As he retreated, the daemon stepped down from the landing. The ragged flesh on its elongated foot sizzled and smoked as it touched the glossy floor, but it didn't faze the monster. Alrik became even more panicked when he saw that the creature appeared unharmed.

'Crystallised acid!' the duardin said as he climbed back onto the landing. 'The entire floor's coated in it.'

'Well, it isn't stopping the thing!' Bruno shouted.

Alrik gave him a dark look. 'Then I'll find something that will.' He hurriedly pulled off his boots and prodded the two men back towards the last chamber.

Bernger felt his heart racing when he moved out into the silent corridor. He recalled what Alrik had claimed, how sound was the trigger for this trap. *Anything louder than a heartbeat.* What about a heart that was hammering inside his chest like an orruk war drum?

Bruno was already halfway across, shuffling his feet as rapidly as he dared. Bernger followed after his father. He imagined they must look absurd, shoes clenched in their hands, their bare feet sliding along the floor. He struggled to repress the laugh that threatened to crack the silence. He was losing control, letting the panic overwhelm him. He focused on Bruno, fixated on the fact that if he did lose control he would be killing his father too.

When he reached the landing, Bruno dropped his shoes and turned back to Bernger. He waved his son onwards, desperation on his face. Bernger restrained the impulse to look back and see the thing that had provoked such terror. He kept moving, his entire perspective limited to just the landing and the end of the silent hall.

At the landing, Bruno wrapped his arms around his son. Both men then focused their attention back on the room they had escaped. Alrik had stopped midway. The cogsmith was watching the other side of the hall. Approaching him, the sound of its scorched footfalls failing to activate the trap, was the Mardagg. Bernger noticed now the tattered strips of cloth that hung from the daemon, all that remained of Brond's clothes. The gangly monster reached out with one of its long arms as it drew nearer to Alrik.

The duardin stood his ground before the daemon. Bernger could not see Alrik's face, for he had his back to the two men, so he could not be certain what the cogsmith's intention was when he raised his arms and brought his hands together in a loud clap.

Immediately after the sound, there was the rumble of machinery set into motion. From the roof, a great knife came scything down. Fastened to a long iron armature, it swept across the hall like a murderous pendulum. Bernger saw now the manner in which Goswin had died. The blade struck Alrik, slashing through him like a cleaver through a piece of mutton. The duardin was spilt from scalp to groin, his bisected halves flopping obscenely to either side. The crescent-shaped knife continued its butchering swing and slashed into the daemon's monstrous body. The wet, glistening bones and crimson flesh were ripped asunder, cleft apart by the pendulum. The size of the daemon made the cut more jagged than it had been for its other victims and the skull-like head was whole when the creature collapsed to the floor. Bernger could see its ravenous eyes fixed on Alrik's body. Even with such a mutilating wound, the fiendish vitality endured for a moment. Then the same rapid disintegration that had consumed Reiner's possessed figure settled across what had been Brond.

'He killed it!' Bernger shouted.

Bruno shook his head. 'It didn't have prey to hunt. So it left to find another host. And another victim.'

* * *

Climbing down the secret passage from the trophy room, Magda could hear Roald's voice rising from below. 'Then we are in agreement?' the baron said, followed by a muttered reply from Hartmann that she couldn't catch. 'You understand what you have to do?' Roald asked.

Magda motioned for Klueger to hang back so that they might eavesdrop on the baron. Whatever the nobleman was up to, she was certain it wasn't anything intended to benefit anyone else. In the dark, however, Klueger missed her cue and continued on into the cellar. The moment Roald saw him, the previous conversation was set aside.

'Ah, so here you are,' Roald said. 'We have been waiting here for the others. Keeping watch.' He gave a sideways glance at Hartmann. The fat merchant nodded and confirmed the baron's statement.

'We were told everything that happened,' Klueger said. He shifted his gaze from Roald to the trapped room beyond the cellar. 'How long have they been gone?'

Roald didn't have a precise answer to that question. 'It seems like a great deal of time, but not even close to how long it took for Reiner to completely change.'

'There's no knowing how long it took for Reiner to change,' Magda said. 'We don't know how long the daemon waited in the sepulchre for Notker to arrive in the chapel.'

'The aelf Abarahm may be right in another respect,' Klueger added. 'The daemon may not take as long to manifest each time. It's certainly a daemon of Khorne, and as such it will be invigorated by bloodshed. The more violent death that occurs inside Mhurghast, the more firm its presence in Chamon will become. Each possession will come easier than the last, each manifestation faster than the one that preceded it.'

'Then it may already be too late for them to stop the daemon?' Magda asked.

Klueger paused. Magda could tell he was trying to find a way to soften what he would say. 'Even if they destroy the host, they can't destroy the daemon. It will simply find another vessel for its evil.'

Magda felt the pommel of Ottokar's sword against her palm. She thought of Bruno and how his treachery had maimed Ottokar. Though she knew it was foolish and selfish, she was worried that the daemon would cheat the Freeguild captain from a long overdue reckoning.

'Is there no hope then?' Hartmann moaned. 'Even if they destroy the daemon's body?'

'Perhaps a slight one,' Klueger said. 'But it's best to wait and learn.' He checked the charge on his pistol and faced the dungeon.

Magda aimed the weapon Klueger had given her. Even when Bruno and Bernger appeared at the far end of the corridor, she kept the pistol trained on Bruno. It would be so easy to pull the trigger and send a bullet smashing into his arm the same way his assassin had struck down her father. She resisted the urge. Another time, another place, she told herself, she would not hesitate. Grudgingly, she lowered the pistol as the Walkenhorsts hurried towards the cellar.

'We were too late,' Bernger gasped as he joined them. 'The daemon was already manifest in Brond. It came after Alrik.'

'Did it get him?' Hartmann asked.

Bruno shook his head. 'No. The cogsmith lured it into one of the traps. He used himself as bait to draw it in. A big knife that swung down from the ceiling. It cut clean through Alrik and then on into the daemon.'

'That stopped it though,' Roald laughed, though there was a suggestion of nervousness in the sound. 'Otherwise you wouldn't have made it back.'

'I'm not sure,' Bernger confessed. 'When it fell, the daemon started to dissolve. It melted. The same way it did in the chapel after it killed Notker.'

Magda found that she couldn't take her eyes off Bruno. Though she'd lowered the pistol, she kept a ready grip on her father's sword. 'What did you do?' she demanded. 'Did you try to help, or did you just watch?'

'We couldn't help,' Bruno said. 'The slightest sound would have been enough to trigger the knife. All we could have done would be to die with him.'

'The traps – before he died, Alrik showed you how to get past the traps!' Roald had lost whatever reserve he still had.

Bernger answered the baron. 'We learned the secret to getting through the four rooms Alrik took us through. He didn't say if there were more. When he reached the fourth room we met... it.'

'It makes no difference,' Klueger said. 'No one is leaving this castle. Not until it's stopped.' There was sorrow in his eyes when he looked at Magda. 'In Mhurghast the fiend is contained. If it were to get loose in Ravensbach, the havoc it could wreak would be incalculable.'

'I think Brond intended to save his father by killing himself before the daemon could manifest,' Bernger told the witch hunter.

Magda was still watching Bruno. 'Maybe the reverse would be true. Without a victim to hunt, the daemon would not be drawn to the host Count Wulfsige picked for it.'

'Either's possible,' Klueger said. 'The ritual the count performed appears complex. Occult links binding sequences together. Break one link and the sequence falters.'

A strange look came upon Bruno. Magda saw a weird light leap into his eyes. She saw his jaw tighten. Before she knew what was happening, he turned around and darted into the dungeon.

Bernger was slow to understand, but when he did, his shout echoed through the cellar. 'No!'

'Stay there,' Bruno warned. His eyes swept across all of them. 'Keep my son safe. He's the only one who knows how to get past the traps now.'

Magda grabbed Bernger before he could rush into the dungeon. She struggled to hold him back. Before he could break free, Klueger was helping her. Then Roald joined in and the struggling youth was borne to the floor.

'Don't!' Bernger howled. 'Stop him! Stop him!'

Magda could see a kind of regretful pride in Bruno's face as he looked at his son one last time.

'I'm breaking the chain,' Bruno said. Then he stamped his foot down.

CHAPTER VIII

Magda slid her hands across the hilt of Ottokar's sword, savouring the feel of the rough grip against her palms. It was a link between daughter and father, a reminder of who he had been. In her ears she could hear his voice – only slightly slurred by drink – encouraging her to greater discipline in her swordsmanship. Pain flashed through her, pulsating from her heart down into her very toes. The sense of loss was almost overwhelming. Unlike Inge, she'd never stop loving Ottokar. She wondered if that meant the pain she was feeling now would never go away.

Across the parlour, the others were talking. It was happenstance, but she found her gaze focused on Bernger. She could see the hurt he was suffering. It was etched on every line of his face. His anguish was only too familiar. He'd lost his father, right before his eyes. Helpless to act but at the same time blaming himself for not doing something to stop it. Magda felt ashamed that she couldn't muster any regret over Bruno's death. There should be something, but there wasn't. She didn't repent the hate she'd felt for the man. She wondered though if she would have felt any satisfaction if it had been her sword rather than the dungeon's trap that had put an end to Bruno. Because as things stood, there was only emptiness.

'The duardin are gone,' Klueger stated as he paced before the guests. 'If there was any question about the horrible rite Count Wulfsige performed, there's none now. The Mardagg has been called up from the Blood God's infernal kingdom. It will infest those who ate the profaned food and drew into themselves the mark of Khorne. Then it will use these hosts to murder their parents.' It was a mark of the witch hunter's agitation that he didn't shun the use of the profane names, as though by speaking them he could defy the power of the beings they represented.

Magda saw the fear that shone in the eyes of the older guests. They cast anxious looks at their own children, horrified by their presence. Even Saskia Krebs stirred from her dreamy indifference to stare at her son, Thilo, as though he were some venomous reptile. Magda felt her heart sag when she saw the same fear in Inge's face. Her mother tried to muster a reassuring smile, but it looked devoid of emotion. A mask adopted to hide her inner dread.

'There is more,' Lothar told Klueger. 'Something perhaps none here have considered.' The alchemist pointed to Abarahm. 'Your mother, did she love you?' The aelf slowly nodded. Lothar turned to Bernger. 'And there can be no mistaking the intention of your father when he... died.'

'What are you saying?' Hiltrude demanded. She pulled her hand away when Roald tried to grasp it. 'What are you saying, you filthy poisoner!'

Lothar shrugged at the insult. 'You should thank me for that *poison*, as you call it. Perhaps you would already be dead if you had more children for the daemon to choose from. More tickets in this lottery of death we have all been condemned to.'

Abarahm rose from his chair and regarded Lothar with an icy stare. 'Why did you ask how Nushala felt about me?'

'Because he thinks it was more than arrogance that made her walk out into the courtyard,' Magda suggested. 'He thinks she deliberately provoked them into killing her.'

'That's horrible!' Inge cried out.

'It is absurd,' Hiltrude scoffed.

Lothar shook his head. He turned towards Klueger. 'What do you think? Horrible, I agree, but absurd I do not. There was purpose in these deaths. Not simple self-destruction, but self-sacrifice.'

'The daemon would spare a potential host if there was no victim associated with them,' Klueger said.

Magda slid across the divan and grabbed hold of her mother. She felt Inge tremble in her grasp. They locked eyes. She wondered if her own gaze held the same expression of horror that she saw in Inge's. All she could do was hold on to her and shake her head, desperate to keep the thought from her mother. She remembered what her parents had said, that they would do anything to protect her.

'Monstrous,' Hiltrude said, her voice choked as she blurted the word.

Roald echoed her sentiment, if not her tone. 'Is there logic behind this vile speculation, or is it simply depraved imagination?' He directed a sideways glance at Hartmann, a stern look that the merchant couldn't hold.

'Magic obeys certain laws in order to manifest in the Mortal Realms,' Lothar said. 'Even the blackest sorcery drawn from the Realm of Chaos must be subject to rituals and incantations, limitations that confine and focus its dark energies.

Conjuring the daemon has shaped aetheric chains to sustain its presence. One of those chains is Mhurghast. The castle itself is a boundary for the daemon. Another is the vindictive bonds described by the count when he summoned the fiend. It possesses a host and then hunts a victim. These too are chains.'

'And if the chain is broken,' Bernger said. 'If the father dies then the son is spared?' Magda could hear the guilt in his voice.

Klueger rapped his fist against the wall in a gesture of frustration. There was fury in his eyes when he answered. 'I don't know,' he admitted. 'I don't know if Bruno and possibly the aelf as well died for a noble purpose or a useless... I just don't know. This daemon's unlike anything I have encountered before.'

'But if the link between parent and child is broken,' Roald said, 'then won't that confound the fiend's ability to manifest?'

'It will,' Lothar declared, 'but I do not know to what degree. It may simply mean that once the daemon has killed all of its designated victims, it will still possess those who are left behind.' He bowed apologetically to Abarahm. 'It could simply mean that instead of escape, you get put at the back of the line.'

Magda gave a start when Hartmann suddenly lunged to his feet. The merchant moaned in horror. He waved his hands in the air and cried out to the other guests.

'What good does it do to sit here and babble on and on?' Hartmann wailed. He swung around and pointed his trembling hand at Herlinde and Heimo. 'The daemon's looking for a new host. Any moment now it could take over one of our children just as it did Brond!' He glanced back at Klueger. 'You're supposed to know how to protect people against this evil. Why aren't you doing something?'

'Herr Senf, that is enough,' Hiltrude barked.

Hartmann shuddered under the authority of the baroness and retreated back into his chair.

Klueger looked across the parlour. His eyes lingered on Magda. She could tell that he had reached some sort of a decision, but when he gazed at her he hesitated. Whatever he had in mind, Magda was prepared to trust him. She gave the slightest nod, hoping none of the others would notice.

'We'll do something,' Klueger said. 'Mhurghast's a big place. There are many rooms on the floors above us. As we don't know who'll be chosen to act as the daemon's host next, those who are threatened will be confined. Each in a separate room.'

Roald took up the suggestion with evident excitement. 'I have been in the castle many times. Each of the bed chambers can be locked from the outside.' He adopted a contemptuous look. 'The count was always suspicious of visitors and didn't want them wandering around at night.'

'Then we'll make use of those rooms,' Klueger said. He smiled apologetically at Magda. 'They are unlikely to be in readiness, but you'll forgive the discomfort.'

Abarahm scowled at the witch hunter. 'You do not mean to confine me.' Despite the melodic lilt in the aelf's voice, there was a threat in his words.

Klueger managed to surprise Abarahm by lowering his right arm to display the pistol gripped in his left hand. 'That's exactly my intention. One way or another.'

Lothar walked over to the aelf. 'Be sensible,' he advised. 'We are not certain if you are still menaced by possession. Do as the witch hunter says.'

Abarahm's scowl deepened. 'It is an affront upon my dignity.'

'If I am going to confine my only daughter, then I do not want to hear about an aelf's dignity,' Roald snapped.

The remark brought Liebgarde to her feet. Shock was on her face. 'You can't mean to lock me away, papa!'

Hiltrude moved to comfort her child. 'Of course not, dear. No one is making you go anywhere.' She cast a challenging glare at Klueger.

'With deference to your rank, your ladyship,' Klueger said, 'Liebgarde will be confined just like all the others.' Magda knew he was thinking of her when he added, 'None of us wants to consider where this fell spirit may strike next.'

'Then I am going with her,' Hiltrude declared. 'I will not have my daughter left alone to the horrors of this castle.'

Roald knelt beside the baroness. 'Be sensible. What if Klueger's right and our daughter is the next–'

Hiltrude's eyes blazed like a raging fire. 'Von Woernhoers do not turn into monsters! Liebgarde is a von Woernhoer. A von Woernhoer by blood, not marriage!' She swung around and returned her gaze to Klueger. 'If you insist on imprisoning my child, then I am going with her.'

Klueger nodded. 'If that's your intention, know that I'll be incapable of protecting you.' He turned to the other guests. 'If any of you want to stay with your children, I'll not stop you. But I will warn you. When the daemon comes, you may be placing yourself right beside it.'

Magda shivered. The daemon would come. When it did, who would be next to feel its evil growing inside them? Bernger? Liebgarde? Heimo? Herlinde?

Or would it be Magda Hausler?

The room Bernger found himself in was spacious. Once it might have been described as opulent, but there was a patina of decay everywhere. The blackwood panelling was chipped and splintered from the attention of rats. There was a musty smell about the bedding, and the golden frame had lost its glitter beneath layers of dust. The flue in the fireplace was caked in soot, and smoke seemed reluctant to be drawn up into it. The sheet that covered the heavy chair near the room's narrow window had been there so long that when he went to pull it away he stripped a layer of paint from the arms.

Every instinct inside the thief told Bernger to rebel against his confinement. When Klueger was moving to lock the door, he felt an urge to rush the witch hunter. But these impulses to seek freedom were not strong enough to penetrate the despair that numbed his brain. Bruno was dead. He had died to protect his son. Now it appeared his sacrifice might have been in vain.

'What do you think it feels like?' Bernger asked Klueger. 'What'll it be like when the daemon comes?'

Klueger paused at the door. 'Possession can be an insidious thing. It steals upon a person without their knowing. At first it's subtle. A strange thought, an alien idea. Then, when the daemon's essence gains a firmer hold, wild impulses will seize the host. Strange thoughts become stranger actions. The personality of the host is perverted by these influences. The more the soul strays from the usual custom, the more the daemon twists it. Twists it until it breaks and there's nothing left.'

'Then it doesn't start with the physical change?' Bernger pointed to his eyes, reminding Klueger of Reiner's and Brond's blood-filled orbs.

'No. By the time there's a physical symptom, the daemon has already taken hold.'

Bernger shook his head. 'That means it could already have chosen its next host.' He thumped his hand against his chest. 'Even when my father was... Even at that moment, the fiend might already have been inside me.'

Klueger did not mince words. 'Possible,' he agreed. 'The moment it left Brond's flesh it would have been seeking its next vessel. That's why all who were marked have to be confined. None of us knows who could be next.' The witch hunter glanced at the right wall, in the direction of the room where Magda was held. Bernger saw something akin to panic in Klueger's eyes. 'With a lesser daemon, there are tests and trials that could reveal its presence from the first moment. The Mardagg is not so easily exposed. It's among the Blood God's great daemons and is not without its own profane protections. We're not helped that the fiend is more subtle than most that serve Khorne.'

'How do you mean?'

'Most of Khorne's daemons expend themselves in reckless bloodshed and carnage. They're entities of the moment, immediate and terrible in their havoc. This one's different. It can be infernally patient and bide its time if it anticipates the opportunity for an even greater slaughter in the future. I think Ravensbach is almost fortunate that Count Wulfsige restricted its attentions as he did.'

Bernger turned to the narrow window and looked at the lights of the town below the hill. 'What'll it do once it has done everything the count summoned it to do?'

'That's a question I fear to consider,' Klueger confessed. 'It uses its hosts, but it draws no energy from them. Those it kills are different. The life force of those killed by the daemon will empower it, lend it a firmer presence in Chamon. If that power grows great enough, it may break free from the count's designs. Should that happen, none will be safe. The "chains" Lothar speaks of would be utterly broken. It would be able to go where it liked and butcher whoever it came upon.'

'I understand,' Bernger said. 'There's far more at risk here than just ourselves. You did the right thing to confine us.' He shook his head. 'If we're confined, then you'll be able to subdue the daemon when it first tries to manifest. When it may still be weak.'

'That's my intention,' Klueger said. 'I'll keep watch in the hall outside. The Order of Azyr has trained me to be sensitive to the presence of daemons. When it begins to take control of its host, I'll know and I'll be in position to act.'

Klueger started to leave the room, but turned before closing the door. 'The traps Alrik showed you...'

'I've told you all I know about the way they operate and how to get past them,' Bernger said. 'I can explain them again if you need me to, though Baron von Woernhoer or Hartmann might know as much as I do at this point.'

'Yes, they were very attentive to your report,' Klueger said, a grim smile flickering across his face. 'But it wasn't about the traps the cogsmith told you about. It's the ones that could be deeper in the dungeon. The ones that are still unknown.'

Bernger thought he understood Klueger's problem, but he could see no way to help him. 'I only know about the first four rooms.'

'Indeed,' Klueger said. 'But – you'll forgive me – you're known to have some ability when it comes to getting around traps. Bernger Walkenhorst's professional activities aren't unknown to me.'

'A delicate way to express it.' Bernger bowed to the witch hunter.

'I have little time for delicacy. What I want to know is this – do you think you saw enough in the mechanisms Alrik *did* show you to figure out how other ones might work?'

'Use the known to predict the unknown?' Bernger gave it some thought. He could imagine Bruno looking down at him with disapproval, reproving him for his thievery. 'It's hard to work out how a duardin's mind works. The key to bypassing any trap is knowing the designer's work, and I have seen several examples.'

'Give the problem your attention,' Klueger said as he stepped into the hall and closed the door. 'Lives will depend on it.'

Bernger stared at the door for some time, Klueger's parting words echoing through his brain. It was an onerous responsibility the witch hunter had set upon his shoulders. One that had come to him too late. The life he would have saved was already lost. His own, he felt, didn't really matter. Creatures like Lothar, Hartmann and Roald weren't people who would be missed – Ravensbach would be better without them.

Then Bernger thought of Magda, and his cynicism faltered. She, at least, was someone he would help if he could. He owed it to her for the harm his father had inflicted on Ottokar. Yes, she was someone he would be willing to risk the dungeons for.

Bernger sat down on the edge of the musty bed and pondered Alrik's mechanisms and whatever similarities they shared between them. Anything that might hint at what else the cogsmith had designed for Count Wulfsige.

Roald could hear bats creeping about in the canopy that covered the enormous bed. He was not sure which offended him more, that the chamber to which he'd withdrawn had been neglected to an appalling degree or that even in such decay it was more magnificent than anything in his own home.

The baron pulled his coat tighter, trying to coax some more warmth from the garment. He cast a longing look at the cold hearth. He wanted dearly to light a fire, but he knew he couldn't take the risk. It was reckless enough to have a candle with him, but he wasn't going to wait in total darkness. He'd taken precautions so that the light was shielded from the door. He considered it doubtful that even Klueger would notice anything if he passed by.

There was, of course, the chance that the witch hunter would spot Hartmann, but that was a risk Roald was prepared to take. The fat coward would do his utmost to keep from being noticed, and if he was, well, he wouldn't have to feign fear to sell Klueger on his story about wanting to be close in case there was trouble.

Roald regarded the weapons lying on the table beside the candle. He'd purloined them from the trophy room while Klueger was busy locking up the children. An ugly barbarian mace was his pick. Fashioned from the claw of some reptile, it would leave the sort of rending marks a daemon would be expected to make. The crescent-shaped dagger was Hartmann's. If the fool slashed wildly enough with it, he might make it look like the daemon's work. It mattered little. Once the deed was done, he'd have no more use for Hartmann.

The sound of someone outside the room caused Roald to cover the candle. Every part of his being was alert and focused now, fixated on the door as it slowly opened. He breathed easier when he recognised the short, hefty outline of Hartmann as he slipped into the room.

'Klueger has been patrolling outside the bedrooms,' Hartmann whispered. 'I've been watching him, like you said.'

'Then why aren't you still watching him?' Roald snarled at his confederate. 'We have to watch for our chance. At some point he's sure to visit the girl, Magda. That is when we move.'

The merchant grinned. 'That's why I came to see you. We don't need to wait. Klueger's gone.'

Roald took up the weapons and walked towards Hartmann. 'You're certain? How long's he been gone?'

'Only just now. It's better than you planned. He didn't go to see the woman. He went downstairs.'

The information struck Roald as too good to be true. 'Downstairs? Why would he stop patrolling?' He gave Hartmann a stern look. 'You're certain he didn't spot you?'

Hartmann nodded. 'Positive. He never knew I was there. I watched him from the landing, and he was headed to the parlour.' The merchant chuckled. 'Maybe he required some liquid fortifying for his vigil.'

Roald didn't think that likely. Witch hunters were abstemious to the point of asceticism. Whatever had drawn Klueger to the parlour, it wouldn't be the count's liquor cabinet.

'Come along,' the baron ordered. 'We'll see. If he's gone downstairs, the opportunity is better than I'd hoped for.'

The two men moved out into the darkened hallway. Each carried a candle, warding back the blackness, allowing them to pick their way down the corridor. Roald's ears were keyed to the slightest sound that might betray the witch hunter ascending the stairs. Every step he took, he half expected Klueger to emerge from one of the rooms and confront them.

The first occupied room the men passed was where Thilo Krebs was confined. They could hear the alchemist's son pacing back and forth. Roald imagined it must be a hard thing to bear alone, wondering if at any moment you would lose yourself and become a monster.

'Here,' Hartmann whispered. The next door was the room where the von Woernhoers had been sequestered. To the last, Hiltrude had remained obstinate about not being separated from Liebgarde, so she'd been locked away with her.

Roald stared at the door. He could picture his lovely daughter inside. She would be lying on the bed, her face red from weeping. Hiltrude would be trying to reassure her, though of course the baroness was too dictatorial in her manner to put anyone at ease.

One last chance to stop. Roald recognised that fact. He could turn back now, but for what? To wait until Liebgarde was possessed and the daemon came for him? No, this was what made sense. If the daemon couldn't manifest without a victim to hunt, then it certainly couldn't manifest without a host to possess.

Without a word, Roald handed Hartmann the knife. The baron looked down the hallway to the door of the room where the younger Senfs were confined.

'The baroness?' Hartmann asked.

Roald didn't hesitate to answer. 'Both of them. Come now, Herr Senf. I'll have two lives to my account. It's only fair that you should have the same. You'll need to settle her first, then... then Liebgarde. Make it quick.'

He left the merchant and hurried down the corridor. Roald didn't look back until he was outside the room and had his hand on the key in the lock. Then he glanced over at Hartmann and nodded. They would enter the rooms simultaneously, lest some cry of warning arouse the other targets.

Roald flung open the door and dashed into the room. It was brightly lit by the fire that crackled in the hearth. He saw Heimo turn from warming his hands before the flames. The youth had a bewildered look on his face when he saw the baron. Only at the last moment did he spot the clawed mace in Roald's hand. Heimo threw up his arm to protect himself. Roald struck anyway, the reptilian claws ripping through his victim's flesh.

Heimo stumbled as blood gushed from his torn arm. He fell to the floor and tried to scramble towards the wall. Roald pounced on him like a hunting sabretusk. The barbaric mace smashed the man's head and slashed his scalp. He wilted under the blow, but Roald hit him again and again, bashing his skull until clumps of his brain clung to the saurian claws.

Certain his first victim was dead, Roald spun around to find the second. In his haste, he'd left the door open, a route of escape for Herlinde had she seized upon it. Instead Heimo's sister sat on the bed in open-mouthed horror, completely paralysed by the brutal murder. Only when Roald came at her did she regain something of her senses. She threw herself from the bed and made a dash for the door, a frightened howl escaping her lips.

There was only the one cry. Roald caught Herlinde's hair as she ran for the door. He pulled and dragged her back towards him. The instant she was in reach, he struck at her with the mace. The weapon smacked into her head with such savage force that the claws embedded themselves in her skull. She crumpled to her knees. A garbled moan left her mouth before she pitched face-first to the floor.

Roald tried to tug the mace free, but it was caught fast. He didn't make a second attempt. He was eager to be gone from this den of murder.

Retreating back into the hall, Roald could hear fists pounding against the doors to the locked rooms. The others had heard the sounds of violence, but so long as they hadn't carried downstairs, there was still time to achieve his purpose. The baron ignored the prisoners and rushed to the door Hartmann had opened.

'Hiltrude,' Roald muttered, shocked when he saw the baroness appear in the doorway. She was a horrible sight, her lavish gown drenched in blood. Her neck was deeply gashed, as were her arm and bosom. There was a glazed look in her eyes, for which Roald was grateful. Even as the woman was dying, he was afraid of her.

Hiltrude groped blindly for the wall as she came into the corridor, using it to steady herself. She tried to speak, but all that came from her mouth was a bubble of blood. Though he'd conceived the plot, Roald felt disgusted. Hartmann, in his panic, had proven to be a butcher. The baron backed away from the door. He didn't want to see Liebgarde in such a state.

Hartmann abruptly raced into the hall. The merchant's face was so pallid it might have been sculpted from alabaster. His clothes were even more drenched with blood than

Hiltrude's. He held the dagger in both hands, clasping it close to his breast as though it were a holy icon. The look in his eyes was one of abject terror.

'Baron! Your daughter!' Hartmann tried to run past Roald. The baron had just caught hold of the man when he heard slow footsteps moving through the room Hartmann had fled.

Roald froze in the hallway. A horrible, familiar charnel reek smashed into his senses. It was the smell of carnage far greater than that which he'd just perpetrated. The murderous scent of the daemon.

'We're too late!' Hartmann cried. 'She's possessed!'

It was all Roald could do to pry the dagger from his hands. He tightened his hold on the merchant before risking a look into the room. At once he leapt back. Less than a foot away was the advancing figure of Liebgarde. Or at least something that had been Liebgarde. His daughter's face was contorted into a visage of blood-crazed depravity, her eyes dripping pits of crimson gore. Most awful of all, though, was the unnatural growth. Her body was stretched, her clothes taut against the elongated bones. In places the skin was cracked and split, unable to restrain the ghastly metamorphosis.

'Run!' Roald hissed at Hartmann. He pushed the merchant ahead of him as they fled down the corridor. The baron risked a glance over his shoulder. Some life must have yet lingered in Hiltrude, because Liebgarde had stopped just outside the door to mutilate her mother with fingers that were swiftly becoming talons.

Of all the horrors that shuddered through his brain, the most terrifying were the words Hartmann had used. It was too late. Liebgarde was possessed. That meant that when she was finished with Hiltrude, she would come looking for her father.

* * *

Klueger was aware that he was being watched when he left the hallway and started downstairs. Hartmann was keeping tabs on him. That meant Baron von Woernhoer was somewhere nearby. The two had been thick as thieves since returning from the dungeon. He didn't know what they were planning. At the moment, he didn't care.

The witch hunter walked the desolate halls. Candles lit the path between the stairs and the parlour, but their light did little to offset the grim atmosphere that haunted Mhurghast's passageways. To Klueger it felt like stealing through a mausoleum. The castle had no part with the living. It was a place for the dead.

Sigmar's justice could defy even the hand of Death. Klueger had seen with his own eyes the immortal Stormcast Eternals, divine warriors reborn to serve the God-King, cheating Nagash even as the Great Necromancer reached out to claim them. Yes, the power of Sigmar was absolute if the cause was just.

If the cause was just.

It had been Klueger's lot to do many terrible things as a witch hunter, but always he had felt justified. He did what he did because he did so in the name of Sigmar. To protect the innocent and stamp out the seeds of corruption. He had deliberated on his choices and executed them without bias. The judgement of holy books and sacred teachings informed his actions. Never had selfish interest played a role. Not until now.

Klueger saw the parlour door ahead. He lingered outside for a time, listening for any sound from within. He expected to hear voices. Lothar and his wife, Saskia, should be inside, along with Inge Hausler. Strain his ears as he could, he caught no sound. Briefly he considered turning back from his purpose. Then he heard footsteps inside the room. Someone was walking towards the door.

Inge stepped out into the hall, peering down the corridor in the other direction. She waited a few moments, then turned to go back inside. When she did, she spotted Klueger and jumped back in surprise.

'You startled me,' she said.

'That's the hallmark of a witch hunter,' Klueger replied. 'But in this case I was only able to do so because you were preoccupied.'

Inge nodded. 'I was looking for Herr Krebs and his wife. He wanted to investigate Count Wulfsige's library and took Saskia with him.'

'Then they're not here?' Klueger asked. 'What about Baron von Woernhoer and Herr Senf?'

'They're gone too,' Inge said. 'I don't know where.'

Klueger nodded. 'You're alone. That would explain your nervousness. Mhurghast isn't the sort of place one should be alone in.'

A bit of fire blazed in Inge's eyes. 'Yet you saw fit to lock Magda away by herself. Shouldn't you be up there watching the rooms? Waiting to see... who will be next.'

'It's because of Magda that I came down here to see you.' Klueger removed his hat and held it towards the door. 'What we have to discuss is private. If you would join me in the parlour.' Klueger waited for Inge to precede him. As she walked past, his fingers worked at the lining of his hat, tearing at the felt.

Inge went towards the fireplace. 'I know you have feelings for my daughter,' she said. 'I haven't approved of you. I wanted better for Magda. Someone who doesn't lead such a dangerous life. Someone who would always be there for her. Now all I care about is someone who can just get her out of here. If you can do that, she's yours. With my blessing.'

Klueger stared at Inge's back. He finished plucking the thin cord from under the felt. He wound it between his fingers, feeding it from hand to hand. 'I'll need more than your blessing to save Magda.'

Klueger caught Inge just as she turned towards him. He got the garrotte around her neck and twisted it tight. The woman fought, kicking at him, trying to grasp the cord and pull it away. Fitful gasps rattled up from her throat. She wheezed and coughed as her body tried to draw air into her lungs.

Grimly, Klueger maintained the strangling grip. He kept one eye on the door, watching for any of the others to appear. Every second he was left alone with Inge felt like a gift from Sigmar. An endorsement of the desperate lengths he'd been driven to.

Inge's struggles grew less violent as the strength was choked out of her. Though her face was contorted into a grimace of agony, Klueger thought he saw understanding in her eyes. It was instinct that made her fight him. In her mind and in her soul she knew why this had to be. Why this had to happen.

Klueger was placing all his hopes in the death of Magda's mother, just as Bruno had placed his faith in his own death.

'I'll get Magda out of here,' Klueger told Inge as a ghastly rattle sounded deep in her throat. Her face had taken on a purplish hue. Her eyes rolled back, exposing the whites.

'I'll do whatever it takes to save her,' Klueger vowed.

It took him a moment to realise he was making his promise to a corpse.

CHAPTER IX

Roald hurried through the dark halls of Mhurghast, his pounding feet sending ghostly echoes through the castle. Each turn was met with a feeling of utter dread. He expected to see the thing that had been his daughter waiting for him, its eyes spilling blood down her cheeks, its claws stretched out to rend the flesh from his bones.

'Faster, damn you!' Roald snarled at Hartmann. If Liebgarde was waiting for him, keeping the merchant in front would at least provide some kind of warning.

Hartmann's steps sounded like the thunderous drive of a charging troggoth in the empty corridor. The merchant's back was drenched in sweat, his breath a ragged wheeze. Terror kept him going, forced him beyond the limits of his stamina. Roald was thankful for the man's blind panic. If he took only a moment to think things through, he'd know Liebgarde wasn't after him. Roald was the only prey she was hunting.

How long would Liebgarde linger over Hiltrude? How soon

before she wearied of mutilating the dying baroness? However long, it couldn't be time enough for Roald. Liebgarde might even make Hiltrude's death quick so that she could pursue her other prey.

'The trophy room!' Roald cried out when he saw the doorway ahead. Hartmann turned and ran for the room. The baron let him get a few steps ahead. He watched when Hartmann ducked into the chamber and waited to hear the merchant cry out. When no scream carried back to him, Roald decided it was safe.

Thick shadows hung about the chamber, throwing the suits of armour and display stands into darkness. A few candles had been left burning to either side of the hidden door and the route down to the dungeon. Hartmann stood in the little circle of light, doubled over with his hands on his knees. Roald could hear him gasping for breath, his panic no longer allowing him to ignore the limits of his flabby stamina.

It was actually a good thing, Roald thought. While haste was certainly to be desired, for what lay ahead caution would be even more vital. The less risk there was of Hartmann plunging onwards in unreasoning fright, the better it would be for the baron.

Roald gave a last look back into the hallway. He strained his ears. A faint sound reached him. Was it the patter of rats, or was it something else? Skeletal feet creeping through the castle. A daemon seeking the prey promised to it by a madman.

The baron strode quickly through the trophy room to join Hartmann. He paused only once, stopping before a rack of old spears. He removed two of them and held them under his arm as he continued towards the secret door.

'We need to be going,' he said.

His face flushed with his recent exertions, the merchant shook his head. 'I am all done in. I have to rest.'

Roald glared at Hartmann. 'You'll rest forever if you don't get moving! That monster must already be on my trail. We have to get out of the castle if we're to have any chance at all.' He laid his hand on the merchant's shoulder and urged him towards the tunnel. Hartmann nodded and started down the little passageway.

Light flickered in the cellar below. The room looked just as it had when Roald last gazed upon it. His eyes strayed to the first room of the dungeons. The grisly image of Bruno impaled upon the spiked ceiling rose unbidden to his mind.

The same image must have occurred to Hartmann. He turned back towards Roald. The fat man was shaking, a sick look on his face. 'I can't. I can't go in there.'

'It's the only way out,' Roald said. He took one of the spears and cracked it against the wall. After two tries, he splintered the heft. A third blow expanded the damage enough that he was able to snap off the spearhead by jabbing it against the floor. 'Here,' he said, and handed Hartmann what remained of the pole. 'You can use this to probe your way forwards.'

Hartmann clutched the pole in a desperate grip, but from the way he looked at it the thing might have been a deadly viper. He took a step back. 'You... you want me to... go first.'

'If you get in trouble, I can help you that way,' Roald said.

A light of awareness flashed in Hartmann's eyes. His face contorted into a suspicious leer. Roald appreciated that he'd overplayed his hand. The merchant was only half credulous fool. 'You'd leave me. If there's trouble you won't risk your neck for mine.' The suspicion gave way to realisation. 'You said "the daemon is on *my* trail", not *our* trail! It isn't after me! It's only after you! You killed Herlinde and Heimo. There's no link from me back to the daemon now!'

Cold fury roared through every corner of Roald's being. He pointed the remaining spear at Hartmann, its sharp tip prodding his belly. 'If you'd held to your part of the bargain, there'd be no link between myself and the daemon either. But you didn't, Herr Senf. And now you're going to make amends. You're going to help me get through the dungeon. I know I can trust you to do your best, because both our lives will be at stake.'

Sweat poured down Hartmann's brow. 'I won't,' he insisted. He threw down the pole. 'You can't force me to do it.'

'Can't I?' Roald drove the tip of the spear so that it cut into Hartmann's skin and drew blood. 'You'll do everything I tell you to do or I'll skewer you like a pig. Pick up that pole.'

Roald stepped back while Hartmann leaned over to retrieve the pole. He found himself near the tunnel to the trophy room. Again there came that slow, furtive sound of footsteps. Was it his imagination? He couldn't take that chance.

'Get going,' Roald snapped. He prodded the merchant forwards. Hartmann stopped moving when he saw the bloodstains on the floor in the first room, fed by the drops falling from the ceiling. The baron poked him in the back with the spear. 'Mind your step and don't even think of using that pole. You might need it later, but if I see it so much as dip towards those tiles it'll be the last thing you do.'

Hartmann kept the pole level as he walked across the room. He kept his head down, eyes fixed on the tiles. Such was his wariness of a wrong step that he paused each time he set his foot down, as though waiting for the spikes to come slamming down on their heads. Roald bristled at the exaggerated care and the delay it caused. He kept looking back and wondering if he really could hear something in the secret passage. Either way, he wished Hartmann would move faster.

After what felt like an eternity, Hartmann was across the first room. Roald was quick to join him on the causeway between the count's deathtraps. 'Remember what Bernger said about the next room,' Roald said. 'Keep to the centre, where your weight can be supported. If you try to walk across, you'll just be knocked into the walls and cooked.'

There was no need to remind Hartmann of what they faced. He crawled across the centre of the copper floor, where the hidden beam provided support. If anything, his progress was more agonising than it had been in the first room, but Roald knew he couldn't hurry the merchant. He still needed Hartmann to clear the way. They both knew how the first four rooms functioned. Anything after that would be a mystery, but with Hartmann going ahead of him, Roald would have a chance to see at least a fifth room in operation before having to make his way through it.

The two men had their boots off when they reached the room with the pendulum. Roald had to remind Hartmann to keep his mouth shut when the merchant saw the bisected corpses of Alrik and Goswin. What had been Brond was only a shapeless heap of meat and bone now, corrupted even in death by the infernal touch of the Mardagg.

Warily the two men slid their feet across the floor. Roald kept looking towards the roof, expecting at any moment that some stray sound would provoke the pendulum into action. He listened for the noise of its mechanism grinding into murderous life. It was a different sound that reached him, however. Faint and still distant, it was that of someone stepping out onto the copper floor in the chamber the men had just left. Roald could not hide from the ghastly truth. Liebgarde was pursuing him, and she was now close on his heels.

The fourth room, the last of which Roald knew the secret. Hartmann stuffed his feet into his boots and set off across the acidic floor. Smoke boiled off the soles, but the merchant didn't delay. Any doubt that the sounds he heard were real left Roald. Hartmann's haste could only mean that he also heard them and knew Liebgarde was close behind them.

'Slow down!' Roald barked. He pulled on his own boots and started out into the chamber. The merchant was a third of the way across and rapidly putting distance between them.

'The daemon's after you, not me!' Hartmann shrieked back. 'When it catches you, it'll leave me alone. I can go back! I won't have to risk these traps!'

The mocking words had Roald seeing red. Before he fully appreciated what he was doing, he lifted the spear and cast it at Hartmann. It was a sloppy throw, just enough to graze the fat merchant's side. But even that slight contact caused the graceless man to lose his balance. A scream of horror was ripped from Hartmann as he slammed down onto the floor.

Smoke erupted from the merchant's entire left side. He jerked back to his feet, but it was too late. Some of the floor's oily sheen clung to his skin, burning into his flesh. There was no blood, only a greasy vapour that bubbled off Hartmann as the acid ravenously bit into him. He lost all reason, all sense of direction. In his agonies he staggered around, no longer striking for the landing at the other end of the chamber.

The foul, charnel reek that hit the baron's nose caused him to turn. He couldn't hear the sound of a footfall over Hartmann's agonised screams, but he knew what he would see. When he spun around, the baron's heart felt like a lump of ice in his chest. Standing on the landing that connected the third and fourth rooms was the thing that had consumed his daughter. A few scraps of clothing and wisps of hair were all that were recognisable now as belonging to Liebgarde. Her body had elongated into a giant skeletal figure, blood dripping from the split and shredded flesh. The daemon's grinning skull stared at Roald, its teeth stretched into wolfish fangs. The pools of gore that bubbled in its eye sockets blazed with murderous intensity. The daemon would relish destroying him and sending his soul to the hellish kingdom of Khorne.

The baron raced for the far side of the chamber. He dodged Hartmann as the pain-crazed man lunged for him. Each step sent a shudder through Roald's body, terror making his veins feel as though they were chilled to freezing. His breath came in desperate gasps that never seemed to fill his lungs. His vision blurred, causing him to sway as he hurried for the landing.

Roald threw himself onto the safe causeway. He couldn't believe he'd escaped. It seemed utterly impossible. He'd survived.

Then Roald turned his head. He looked back into the trapped room with its acid-glazed floor. The daemon was moving across it with long, steady strides. It paid no notice to the smoke that boiled off its feet or the way the acid devoured its toes. The fiend kept its hideous gaze upon the baron, indifferent to all else that occurred around it.

Hartmann, insane with pain, actually turned towards the Mardagg and reached out to the daemon. There was no succour to be had. A long, bony hand closed around the merchant's head. A twist of the daemon's wrist and Hartmann's screams were silenced. His head went rolling across the floor, the acid eating away his face and scalp. The decapitated body simply slumped down onto its knees like some warrior priest at his prayers.

Roald turned to flee again, but his eyes caught an object lying just a little distance from the ledge. It was the pole Hartmann had been carrying. When the spear struck him, the merchant had flung the pole across the chamber. Now it lay within easy reach of the baron. Roald took two steps out onto the glazed floor and snatched up the pole. He used his glove to wipe away the glaze, then threw the smoking garment at the approaching daemon. It struck the monster high in the chest and remained there, sizzling against its tautened flesh.

Roald knew the daemon wouldn't be stopped. His only chance was to plunge ahead. He'd use the pole just as he would have had Hartmann do. Probing ahead. Trying to trigger whatever fiendish mechanism Alrik had built.

It was too much to hope that when he turned the corner on the landing he'd see the door leading out of Mhurghast's dungeons. Instead he found a wide corridor with another landing at its far end. Another of the cogsmith's traps. Roald stopped and studied the room. The walls, ceiling and floor were all made of iron, apparently as solid as the battlements of Mhurghast itself.

He tightened his grip on the pole and held it out. Roald remained on the landing as he probed the walls of the room ahead. They felt firm under his examination, with no suggestion of heat or acid or any other deadly instrument. He quickly jabbed at the floor and found it likewise solid. He turned his attention to the ceiling and wondered if the menace lay there. As he lifted the pole to check, the walls suddenly crashed inwards. The pole shattered under the crushing impact. Roald jumped back with the wooden stump clenched in his hands. His eyes were wide with horror. Mashed into paste between moving walls! Such was the fiendish trap Alrik had prepared here.

Knowing the nature of the trap wasn't enough. Roald had to discover the method that activated it if he was to pass through. He watched as the walls slid back into their former positions, but he could see no hint of what had triggered them. Before he ventured onwards, he had to learn. Before his time ran out.

Roald turned around as he heard a scraping sound behind him. He stared in mute horror as the Mardagg hefted itself around the corner. The daemon's feet had been utterly dissolved by the acid glaze, leaving only the leg bones. It supported itself by using its clawed hands to push itself along the walls. The fiend's bloody eyes bore down upon the baron.

Time had already run out.

Roald started to rush into the trapped room, but the memory of those crushing walls made him hesitate. In that instant, the daemon threw itself upon him, its skeletal mass crushing him to the floor. He saw the fanged skull leering down at him. Then the Mardagg opened its hideous jaws and sank its teeth into Roald's chest.

The baron screamed, but his cries did nothing to interrupt the daemon's feast.

Klueger carefully laid Inge's body down on the floor and glanced up at the ceiling. The spikes behind the panel would hide the body for him. Even if it were to be discovered, everyone would believe she'd died trying to escape through the dungeons. That, certainly, was what he needed Magda to believe.

The witch hunter stood on the landing between the first and second rooms. He used a candelabra to activate one of the tiles, tossing the heavy iron implement so it struck one of the triggers. The phoney panel whipped back and the spiked roof slammed down. The points stabbed into Inge's dead flesh, impaling the corpse. Klueger could see the bodies of Bruno and several servants already stuck on the spikes, their faces contorted in the grisly agonies of their deaths.

As he looked upon the bodies, a weird impression came to Klueger. It seemed to him that he could actually hear those tortured cries. When the roof withdrew and carried Inge with it behind the fake ceiling, the sound persisted.

Klueger strained his ears and tried to figure out the source of the strange phenomenon. It was then that his gaze chanced upon the floor.

There was so much blood in the first room that Klueger had failed to notice them, but here there was no distraction from the over-sized, bloody footprints. The daemon had been here! Not in the still recognisable shape of Brond, but in its full and monstrous aspect.

Klueger attended the faint sounds more keenly now. Anguished howls, faint to his ears, but with the way the trapped halls baffled noise, they must be strident enough to carry any distance. Someone was being killed. Perhaps it was the daemon's work.

The pistols Klueger carried were blessed by Grand Lector Sieghard. They had served him well throughout the years. The shot they were loaded with was forged from sigmarite, the holy metal from Azyr with which the arms and armour of the mighty Stormcasts themselves were forged. Each pellet was etched with a prayer on its tiny surface, an appeal to draw the God-King's judgement upon all the foul minions of darkness. The silvered sword he bore was likewise branded with sacred maledictions, orisons of wrath against the creatures of Chaos. Weapons designed to give a mere mortal the ability to fight back against eternal evil.

If his heart were pure and his faith were true. Klueger thought about the woman he'd murdered and his motive for doing so. How pure was his heart? How true was his faith?

Questions that would be answered soon enough. If the daemon was here, Klueger would try to stop it. Vanquishing the fiend was the only way to be certain of saving Magda.

The witch hunter kept a pistol in each hand as he crossed the second room. He moved in perfect silence through the third, braced for the cleaving sweep of the pendulum. Klueger looked over the residue of what had once been Brond and considered the ghastly essence of the daemon. The Mardagg utterly consumed its hosts. He could not let such a fate befall Magda.

The third room, and now the screams were louder than before. He could see a body smoking on the acid-glazed floor. From its bulk Klueger knew the corpse was that of Hartmann. He could guess then whose screams he was listening to from up ahead. Baron von Woernhoer had tried to escape the daemon by finding the dungeon exit. Instead the daemon found him.

Klueger sprinted across the acidic floor, disdainful of the threat to himself. He was intent only upon confronting the daemon before it accomplished its murderous task and its spirit withdrew to another host. When he smelled the obscene, charnel reek, he knew the fiend was near. Such a stench could only come from one of Khorne's daemons.

Upon the landing at the other side of the fourth room, Klueger found the ghastly scene. The Mardagg, its shape now that of a monstrous skeleton, was sprawled across Roald's screaming, blood-soaked body. The fiend's fangs chewed into the baron's chest, stripping gory ribbons from the man. Klueger could see the white of bone showing through the dripping meat.

'Sigmar guide my hand,' he prayed as he aimed his pistols at the daemon. The weapons barked almost simultaneously. The first shot hit the monster's shoulder and exploded it into bony fragments. The second smashed into the fanged skull, punching through the cranium and blasting a hole that removed its nasal cavity and the centre of its upper jaw.

The Mardagg turned and stared at Klueger with its horrible, bloody eyes. Never had the witch hunter felt such malignance before. Not from man or undead, not even from those daemons he had battled in the past. There was an eternity of hate in the creature's gaze, an infinite sea of carnage. The Mardagg was the embodiment of death. Not the inevitable, regimented demise that must come to all things, rather the sudden slaughter and the bloodthirsty havoc of primal savagery. The oldest of all emotions, the sin that smouldered in the lowest reptile. The urge to destroy.

Klueger dropped one pistol and drew his silvered sword. The Mardagg swung at him with its clawed hand, the talons raking through the air only inches from his face. He retaliated, his blade licking across the fiend's fingers. Three of the talons were severed by the blow, a greasy red steam spraying from the wound.

The daemon glared at Klueger. Then it brought its other hand stabbing down into the screaming ruin on which it sprawled. The screams stopped as it crushed Roald's heart.

Klueger didn't bother to attack as the skeletal daemon began to disintegrate and collapse into the sort of grisly mash he'd passed in the pendulum room. The Mardagg's essence was already in transition, leaping from this body into that of its next host. He could accomplish nothing here now.

Klueger recovered his pistol and picked his way back through the dungeon. He was still shaken by the enormity of the power he'd sensed in the daemon. Had he truly harmed it in any way, or had it simply been testing him to see if there was any hurt he could do it?

There was one point in the witch hunter's favour. He was convinced now that the Mardagg was drawn to those who had a link between host and victim. He'd recognised the tattered clothes hanging from the daemon as those worn by Liebgarde, and the victim had certainly been Roald. With Hartmann dead, that meant there was no victim to connect Magda, Bernger, Abarahm and the Senfs. That meant its next host could only be Thilo Krebs.

It would not be murder, Klueger told himself as he ran through the trophy room and back into the castle's gloomy halls. It would be an execution. Thilo's life against those of his parents. Two for one, and perhaps more. He'd be able to put to the test whether breaking the chain would also sever the arcane connection that allowed the Mardagg entry into Chamon. It was something that had to be proven.

Klueger dashed up the stairs towards the bed chambers. He could hear Magda banging her fists against the door to her room. She was in a panic, but the thick door muffled her voice so he couldn't make out the words. He could hear Bernger also pounding against his door. Thilo's and the aelf's rooms were quiet. So too were those of the Senfs and von Woernhoers. He could see that the door to each was open. A hideously mauled body lay in the hall just outside the von Woernhoer room. That, he judged, would be the baroness.

He was more surprised when he looked into the other room and found Herlinde and Heimo dead. A sickening scheme suggested itself now. Klueger understood why Roald and Hartmann had been in the dungeon. They'd conspired to perpetrate the reverse of the plan Klueger had adopted. They would save themselves by killing their children. Only the plot had been too late. The daemon had already possessed Liebgarde.

Klueger turned from the scene of filicide. He checked the charge in his pistol and moved towards the door to Thilo's room. His gaze strayed down the hall to Magda's. Any hesitance left him. He'd already come too far to stop now. He turned the key in the lock and threw open the door. His pistol swept across the room as he looked around for the man he'd come to kill. At least,help me

if Thilo was still human enough to kill.

There was only silence. No cry of surprise from Thilo, no

yell for help. The reason was simple. Thilo wasn't in his room. Klueger made a quick search, but there was no sign of him. Somebody had released the alchemist's son. Or else the daemon had found some way of releasing its new host.

Klueger hurried back into the hall. He dashed across to Bernger's room and unlocked the door. The thief backed away when he saw the drawn pistol, alarm in his eyes.

'Come along,' Klueger said.

'What's happening out there?' Bernger demanded. 'I heard screams. The most awful screams.'

The witch hunter scrutinised Bernger's expression. 'Did you hear anything after the screams?'

'Later,' Bernger said. 'After they stopped I heard doors opening. Somebody was talking, but speaking too low for me to hear what they said. I pounded on the door but they ignored me.' He gave Klueger a sharp look. 'I thought it must be you.'

'It wasn't,' Klueger said. He motioned Bernger into the hall. When he joined him, he gestured with the pistol towards Hiltrude's body. 'The baroness is dead. So are Herlinde and Heimo. I think Hartmann and the baron killed them. They tried to keep the daemon from possessing their children so they'd save their own skins. They were too late. I found both of them dead down in the dungeons. They tried to escape, but the daemon was already inside Liebgarde and chased them down.'

Bernger's face turned pale. He shook his head, staggered by the horror of what he was being told. 'We're dying like flies,' he muttered. 'None of us will make it out of here alive.'

'You'll escape,' Klueger snarled. He pulled Bernger with him towards Magda's room.

When he opened the door, Magda leapt forwards rather than back. She held a candlestick. Only Klueger's quick action kept her from braining him with the improvised weapon, darting aside as she brought it whipping down. Magda dropped the bludgeon in horror at what she'd almost done.

'I didn't know,' she cried. 'I didn't know who was out here. The screams...'

Klueger nodded and took her into his arms. 'It'll be all right,' he assured her. He found the words hard to say. So much had already gone wrong. Life would never be the same again. All that remained was to try and save what was left.

'The screams, what were they?'

Klueger quickly told Magda what had happened, though he left out the real reason he'd been in the dungeons. When he finished he explained what he needed her to do. 'You have to get out of the castle. The daemon has taken Thilo as its next host. I'm certain of that. I don't think it'll be content to simply claim the victims Count Wulfsige designated for it. It knows I can fight it, that Thilo will be its final host. It'll not abandon his body as readily as it did the others. It'll try to use him to slaughter anyone it can reach, because it knows it'll be its last chance to kill.'

'How can we get out?' Magda asked.

'You'll go with Bernger,' Klueger said. 'He has seen for himself how the first four rooms in the dungeon work. I followed his instructions and was able to reach the landing where the daemon killed the baron. Follow him, do what he says, and you'll make it through.' He turned and faced Bernger. 'There is a fifth room, at least. I saw it when I found Roald. There must be some mechanism there, something he had some warning of but wasn't able to get past. If the way had been clear, I don't think the daemon would have caught him.'

Bernger nodded, a grave look on his face. 'At least one more,' he mused. 'It would be an interesting puzzle if our lives weren't being wagered on the solution.'

'If we stay here we're just as dead,' Magda said. Alarm

suddenly filled her eyes. She grabbed Klueger's hand. 'My mother! We can't leave without her!'

Klueger's expression was sombre. 'I've already looked for her. Before I came here to release you both. I couldn't find her.'

Magda frowned. 'Then I can't go. I won't leave her behind. Please, I've already lost my father.'

The worry and agony in Magda's face stabbed at Klueger like a knife. He almost choked on the words that came off his tongue. 'I'll look for her, but I need you to go with Bernger. I need to know that you're safe.' He took her by the shoulders and drew her close. His lips pressed against her mouth. 'There is nothing I wouldn't do to protect you. Believe that. I'll stay and look for her. I'll fight the daemon and keep you safe from it.'

Magda's body was shaking. Klueger could feel her tears against his neck. He looked away and caught Bernger's gaze. He motioned with his head for him to lead Magda away. 'Go with Bernger,' he ordered her as he pushed her from his embrace.

'You'll follow?' Magda asked. There was a severity in her voice that would not be ignored.

'When I have your mother,' Klueger lied. 'I already know the way to get past the first four rooms.' He turned to Bernger. 'When you discover how to get past the fifth room, you can leave instructions for me on the landing.' He reached into his tunic and brought out a short stub of pencil and a small leather-bound book. 'Write down what you learn. I'll follow.' He squeezed Magda's hand. 'I promise I'll follow.'

'Find my mother, Klueger,' Magda begged. 'Save her. Promise me you'll save her.'

'I'll do everything I can,' Klueger vowed. A sudden thought occurred to him, and he glanced at the door to Abarahm's room. 'I'll get the aelf to help me find her. There's no better tracker in all the Mortal Realms than an aelf. But you must hurry now. If Abarahm knows you're trying to get through the dungeon, he may decide to go with you instead of helping me look for Inge.'

The lie was bitter in Klueger's mouth, but it had the desired effect. Magda didn't resist Bernger's efforts to start her down the stairs and lead her off towards the trophy room. He hoped the thief was as smart as he seemed. Certainly of all of them he was their best chance to get around the traps.

Once he was certain Magda and Bernger were gone, Klueger turned towards Abarahm's room. He did intend to fight the daemon, just in case it still had any claim upon Magda. The aelf would make a useful ally in such a fight, if he could be convinced of his own peril.

Klueger knocked at the door, but there was no answer from within. A sense of danger nagged at him, and he had his pistol back in his hand when he turned the key. He stepped into the room. Candles burned on the table near the window, but just as he'd found with Thilo's room, the occupant was nowhere to be found.

Perplexed, Klueger walked back into the hall. As he stepped out from the doorway, he was struck from behind. A cloth was crushed against his face while a steely grip clamped down on his wrist and kept him from using the pistol. He fumbled with his other hand to draw another weapon, but the pungent smell of the cloth was already numbing his senses and draining the strength from his limbs. He thought of Alrik and the way Lothar had subdued the duardin.

The witch hunter's legs buckled beneath him and he wilted to the floor. His attacker flowed downwards with him and kept the drugged cloth against his nose and mouth. As his mind started to fade into darkness, Klueger was surprised by the identity of his foe. It wasn't Lothar. It was Abarahm.

From the intensity of the aelf's gaze, Klueger had the impression Abarahm would have been happier using a knife than Lothar's stupefying vapours.

CHAPTER X

'I do not understand why you want him alive.'

Abarahm's voice cut through the darkness that had enveloped Klueger's mind. He tried to move, but found that his hands were tied behind him. He was sitting on a chair and the cords were fastened to its back to hold him in place. Carefully he tested his legs, but they too were bound and connected to the chair.

'Contingency.' The answer came in the sardonic purr of Lothar Krebs. 'If this doesn't work, we may need him.'

Klueger opened his eyes slowly as he tried to hide the fact that he was awake from his captors. He saw that he was in the dining hall. Candles and lamps blazed everywhere. The chair to which he was bound was pushed up near the wall, only a few yards from the door to the corridor outside. The other chairs had been removed from the table, thrown aside in disarrayed heaps. Plates and cutlery, glasses and uneaten food were likewise strewn about the floor. The head of the table, where Count Wulfsige had opened his own throat and used his own blood to summon the Mardagg, was beyond Klueger's field of vision. It was from that direction that the voices came.

'This is the best way. The only way to be sure,' Lothar declared. 'If not, we will have to make a fight of it. That is why we need the witch hunter.'

With excruciating slowness, Klueger started to turn his head to face Lothar. Perhaps the motion would have been gradual enough to escape the alchemist, but the keen eyes of the aelf caught him almost immediately. Abarahm stalked over and seized Klueger by the chin. His slender fingers forced the witch hunter to look at him.

'Klueger is awake,' Abarahm told Lothar. 'Are you sure you still want him alive?' There was an impersonality to the question that made Klueger's blood run cold.

Lothar came away from the end of the table. Klueger could see now that Thilo was chained to the throne-like seat that had served the count. Thick loops of steel were coiled around his body, circling his arms and chest, even his throat and forehead. All that Thilo could move was his eyes. These, Klueger saw, had already turned to pools of blood. The daemon was inside its new host.

'You are wondering, no doubt, what I am doing.' Lothar paced before Klueger. The witch hunter's brace of pistols was belted around his waist. A sideways glance showed him that Abarahm had his sword.

'Heresy,' Klueger said. 'Daemonology. What you're doing is obscene. Unforgivable.'

Lothar smiled and nodded. 'All true,' he conceded. 'But you may also add "necessary" to your description. Desperate moments demand desperate measures.' A cruel laugh rippled from the alchemist. 'I don't think I need to explain that to you. Abarahm tells me you released Bernger and Magda. How did it feel, lying to the woman you love?'

Klueger kept all emotion from his voice when he answered. 'I didn't lie. If that eavesdropping aelf hadn't waylaid me, I would even now be looking for Inge Hausler.'

'That should be easy.' Lothar laughed. 'Since you know where you put her body.'

A gesture from Lothar had Abarahm grab Klueger's chin and force the witch hunter to look at the table in front of Thilo. He was stunned by what he saw. Saskia was sprawled there, lying over the spot that had been stained by the count's cursed blood. Around her had been drawn a pentacle, and the woman's head and limbs stretched away into each point of the design. There was a dazed, dreamy look in her eyes, even more pronounced than her usual stupor.

'You see, we searched for Inge ourselves,' Lothar said. 'She could have helped... bolster... the ritual I have in mind. Abarahm went looking for her. An aelf is very good at finding people, you know.'

'Maybe she's just better at hiding than he is at finding,' Klueger said, pulling his chin free from Abarahm's grip.

Lothar shook his head. 'I think not. You released Magda and Bernger, but you went into Thilo's room with the intention to kill. Abarahm watched you. Why go to kill my son but free the others? It can only be because you accept the theory of arcane chains. That the daemon is irrevocably bound to the pattern of host and victim. Even in your affection, I don't think you'd send the daemon to run amok through Ravensbach. That means you considered Magda as safe as Bernger. The only way that could be is if her mother is dead.'

The witch hunter struggled against his bonds. To have his crime known by a creature like Lothar was too much to bear.

'I don't blame you,' Lothar said, and laid a consoling

hand on Klueger's shoulder. 'The things we do for love can often flirt with madness.' He waved his hand towards Saskia. 'My dear wife wearied of life when she couldn't have more children. I caught her...' He hesitated, a look of remorse briefly on his face. His eyes flashed with a terrible resolve when he glanced again at his possessed son. 'To prevent her from trying again, I gradually conditioned her to a certain potion.' He reached into a pocket and withdrew a silver flask. 'A few drops in her milk, in her tea, in her soup. After a few weeks, she was addicted. She felt listless and weary, but she no longer desired death. You see, she *needed* me again. Only I could give her the mixture that had become life itself.'

As Lothar spoke, Saskia showed the first sign of motion. She turned her head and looked at the flask. The expression in her eyes was of the most abominable lust Klueger had ever seen, a hunger that transcended flesh and rooted itself in the very soul.

Klueger could not look at the ravenous appeal in Saskia's eyes. He turned instead to Lothar. 'A damned heretic! A foul slave of Chaos!'

Lothar sneered at him. 'Like any fanatic, everything must be termed in absolutes. I am no worshipper of the Dark Gods. There are ways to harness the tremendous arcane energies they represent, however. You can exploit Chaos without submitting to it.'

'I've heard those same words from many a witch and sorcerer before they were consigned to the flames.' Klueger glanced at Abarahm. The aelf was fingering the pommel of the silvered sword. 'Your confederate doesn't appear happy with this kind of talk.'

'Abarahm understands that I am the only chance he has to be free from the daemon,' Lothar said. He gave Klueger a solemn look. 'I may be wrong. Even with the links broken, it could still try to consume the hosts prepared for it.'

'Why waste time gloating over this man?' Abarahm asked. 'When you are finished he will die anyway.'

Lothar bristled at the interruption. 'There is still time. Go and watch Thilo if my conversation bores you. Let me know when he begins to weep.' He waited for the aelf to walk away before turning back to Klueger.

'If I could trust you, I wouldn't need to kill you,' Lothar said. 'You know now that I have delved into forbidden lore. I will show you that it has been to a good purpose. What is more, I know about the murder you have committed. The authorities won't take my word against yours, but if it should reach Magda's ears... well, I don't think you would care for that.' He smiled and glanced back at Abarahm. 'Don't worry about the aelf. Whatever happens, he won't say anything. Are we in accord then? Will you swear to Sigmar that neither by action nor word will you move against me?'

Klueger looked past Lothar to where Thilo sat chained in his chair and Saskia lay sprawled upon the table. 'What are you planning to do?'

'I've said that we do drastic things for love,' Lothar began. He reached into his coat and drew out a gruesome-looking dagger. 'This is the phurba the count used to sacrifice himself. This instrument is what made his revenge possible. It called the Mardagg from the Realm of Chaos. With this, I can call the daemon.' His face drooped as he gazed at his family. 'Thilo is already lost to me. Even if the Mardagg were exorcised, now that it has been inside him all that would be left would be a blood-mad maniac. However, I can draw the daemon out. I can send it into Saskia's body.'

'And you say this is done for love?' Klueger scoffed.

'The strongest love of them all,' Lothar said. 'The love of

life itself. To save my own, I must sacrifice others. Quite literally in this case. To continue, Saskia is a perfect receptacle for the daemon. Her body is plagued by a most terrible hunger. The Mardagg consumes the minds of memories of those it possesses. When it possesses Saskia, it will also possess her addiction. It will become as she is, utterly subservient to whoever can feed that addiction.'

'You're mad to think you can control the daemon,' Klueger sneered. 'It'll destroy you and pick its fangs with your bones.'

The alchemist glared back at Klueger. 'It will work. I can render the fiend insensate. Harmless.'

'The tears have begun,' Abarahm called from the head of the table. The aelf backed away from Thilo and drew the silvered sword from its scabbard.

Lothar held the phurba to Klueger's throat. 'Your answer. Quickly.'

'I agree,' Klueger said.

Lothar pressed the dagger against his skin. 'Not enough,' he said. 'Say the words. Swear to Sigmar, and tell the God-King what you swear to do.'

Rage boiled inside Klueger, but pragmatism won the moment. Dead, he could do nothing to oppose Lothar. Alive, there might be a way to stop him and still honour his vow to Sigmar. 'I swear by Ghal-Maraz and to Mighty Sigmar that neither by deed nor word will I bring harm to Lothar Krebs.' He strained against the cords that held him to the chair. 'Now release me.'

Lothar shook his head. 'After,' he said. 'Once the ritual is performed.' Furtively, he looked aside at Abarahm. He removed a slender knife from his belt. 'When I cut you, cry out,' he whispered, his voice so low that the words scarcely made any sound at all. Klueger nodded, though he didn't understand what the alchemist was up to.

'We needed Inge's blood to bait the Mardagg,' Lothar lectured, raising his voice. 'Since you have made that impossible, I will use yours instead.' He raked the knife along Klueger's left arm. The cut was shallow, but deep enough to draw blood. The witch hunter yelled in feigned agony and struggled at his bonds. Lothar leaned close to him. The bloodied knife was replaced on his belt, and he removed a little copper bottle. He made a show of gathering Klueger's blood, but none actually entered the vial.

'Are you finished with him?' Abarahm shouted. There was an edge of panic in the aelf's voice now, distorting its normally melodious quality. 'The tears are flowing faster!' A charnel stench began to fill the room.

Lothar turned and walked towards the end of the table. He held the empty vial in one hand and the phurba in the other. 'I have enough. The woman would have been better, but the witch hunter's blood will suffice.'

Abarahm looked from Thilo to Saskia. 'You are certain you can control it?'

'I am certain,' Lothar assured him. 'There is only one thing that could give us any problems now.'

If Abarahm hadn't been distracted by Thilo's possession, his aelfish speed would have allowed him to react when Lothar made his move. As things stood, the first he was aware of Lothar's treachery was when the phurba was buried in his heart.

Lothar knelt beside his betrayed confederate, the vial pressed to his wound, gathering the aelf's blood. 'Human blood is good bait, but that of an aelf is even better,' he told Klueger. 'Their kind are rare, and so their blood holds an exotic flavour for the daemons of Khorne.'

'You planned to betray him from the start,' Klueger accused.

'It is an unwise man who does not hedge his bets,' Lothar

replied. He rose and walked to the table with the vial. 'The Mardagg might have ignored human blood, since it is already surrounded by what is inside Thilo's body. But it will respond to aelfish blood.' He leaned over Saskia and pressed his finger to the mouth of the vial. With his finger stained crimson, he began daubing streaks across his wife's face.

Klueger watched the profane ritual, but soon his gaze was drawn away from Lothar and Saskia. He looked at Thilo. It could not be his imagination. He was larger now, filling more of the chair. The chains that bound him were stretched tighter than they had been. The witch hunter realised the enormous mistake Lothar had made. He wasn't tempting a daemon from the depths of Khorne's kingdom. He was drawing a daemon that was already in the same room. It already had a vessel of flesh to manipulate and use!

'Lothar! Stop! Stop it now!' Klueger shouted.

Lothar looked up in annoyance. The smirk on his face vanished when he heard one of the chains suddenly snap. He spun around and screamed in terror when he saw what was happening behind him. Thilo's limbs were stretching outwards, the flesh peeling back to expose blood-soaked bone. The face was cracking and splitting as the skull beneath swelled, the teeth expanding into sharpened fangs.

The alchemist threw down the copper vial and snatched one of Klueger's pistols from the gun belt. He was staggered by the recoil from the weapon, but his shot was true. The blessed bullets smashed into Thilo's forehead and gouged a crater in the emerging skull. The damage, however, wasn't enough to route the malicious spirit. The Mardagg hungered, and it would not be denied.

'Cut me loose!' Klueger yelled as Lothar scurried away from the table. Another chain snapped, freeing one of the daemon's arms. 'Hurry, there isn't much time!'

For a ghastly moment, Klueger thought the alchemist was going to abandon him, but before he darted out into the corridor, he moved to the chair and slashed the ropes. 'We must run!' Lothar cried, and seized Klueger's arm.

Klueger shook him off. 'I need my weapons,' he said. The alchemist drew back and placed his hands protectively over the remaining pistol. Klueger saw that he'd dropped the other one after shooting the daemon. 'If I'm to fight the thing, I need my weapons!' Without waiting for a response, he snatched the gun from Lothar. 'Get to the trophy room – I'll meet you there.'

'You can't fight that! You have to run!'

The thing that had been Thilo used its claws to rip through the last of its chains. The daemon stood up, its body already a foot taller than it had been. The Mardagg stared down at Saskia. The drug-dazed woman didn't even react to the grisly death that hovered over her.

'Get going!' Klueger snarled as he pushed Lothar out the door. 'I'll meet you in the trophy room.' He watched the alchemist flee and then turned back towards the daemon. The creature was leaning towards Saskia. Her eyes were bleary and unfocused until the long fangs bit down into her cheek and gnashed away at the blood-covered flesh. Then a tortured shriek was ripped from her as abominable awareness shattered her stupor.

Klueger raised his pistol and fired. He'd seen how ineffectual a single shot was against the Mardagg. It was far more efficacious against the daemon's victim. Saskia's screams fell silent. The daemon, intent upon the aelfish blood spattered across her body, was oblivious to the woman's death. Its teeth continued to gnaw at her flesh.

The pistol Lothar had dropped was lying on the floor right where the daemon stood. Klueger reluctantly abandoned it as lost. The silvered sword claimed by Abarahm was almost as unlikely. The aelf's body lay sprawled only a few feet from the feeding daemon. If the Mardagg took any notice of him, it could reach him in a single step.

'Sigmar guard me,' Klueger prayed, and made a dash for the sword. Intent upon Saskia's corpse, the daemon did not even glance at him as he retrieved the weapon. He stood for a moment, the urge to strike the obscene fiend raging through his soul. The sound of the Mardagg's jaws chewing the woman's flesh was too much to endure.

Klueger raised the blade to slash the daemon from behind. It was the thought of Magda that made him hesitate. If he was wrong, if the daemon would still seek the others marked for it, then he might damn her with his attack. While Lothar lived, the Mardagg was bound to Thilo.

Lowering his sword, Klueger ran from the dining hall. He didn't know how long the daemon would linger over Saskia, but he knew where it would go once it was finished. If he could only thwart it from killing Lothar long enough for Magda to escape from the castle, she would be safe from the Mardagg.

Bernger tried not to look at Roald's mangled body, or the fleshy mush that he decided must have been Liebgarde after the daemon abandoned its host. Baron von Woernhoer had been an arrogant and dictatorial person, the kind of victim he would have robbed without the slightest hint of guilt, but there was something obscene about the way he'd died. Perhaps he was only now appreciating the full horror of Count Wulfsige's revenge – using the child to deliver death to the parent.

Magda stared at the gory tableau, disgust and fear etched across her face. 'Don't... don't let me do that to my mother,' she begged Bernger. 'If it comes... If the daemon... just kill me.'

The weariness and defeat in Magda's voice grated on Bernger. He shared her attitude, despite how desperately he tried to cling to hope. It was a fact he wasn't happy to admit to himself. 'We've come this far,' he snapped. 'We're going to make it all the way. We're going to get out of the castle, and then the daemon won't be able to do anything to us.'

Bernger tried to believe his own words, but he knew how hollow they really were. They'd passed through four of Alrik's traps, but those had been comparatively easy. They'd already known how to navigate them. Now they stood before a fifth room, a hallway that had brought Roald up short and allowed the daemon to catch him. Who could say how many more were beyond this one?

'I'm going to move this... mess,' Bernger said. He gripped the splintered pole lying beside Roald's body and used it to slide the carrion back around the corner. While that gruesome spectacle was lying at their feet, he knew it would be impossible to concentrate on the hall ahead of them and whatever trap was hidden there.

When Bernger came back from removing the bodies he found Magda crouched at the edge of the landing. She was staring out into the menacing hall. For a ghastly moment, he thought she was going to dive in. Kill herself the way his father had.

Magda turned at the sound of his approach. She had an intense expression. 'I've been trying to puzzle out the secret of the hall. The only thing I can see are some wooden splinters on the floor.'

Bernger came forwards and squatted down beside her. She pointed out the debris on the floor. The colour reminded him of the pole he'd used to move the bodies. He went back and got it, ignoring the bloody residue that clung to it. 'Roald must have used this to trigger the trap,' he mused. 'He was still trying to figure out how to get past it when the daemon caught him.'

'But he didn't find a way across,' Magda pointed out. A shudder passed through her. 'He died right here.'

Bernger laid a reassuring hand on her shoulder. 'We're smarter than the baron was,' he said. 'He had other people do everything for him. We know how to do it for ourselves.'

Neither of them spoke while Bernger studied the scene. The splinters on the floor. The way the pole was broken. He glanced at the ceiling in the hall. No, if it had come crushing down, the pole would have snapped with a less ragged break. He turned his attention to the walls. He could just about see a few slivers of wood pressed into them.

'That's the trap,' Bernger declared. He pointed to the slivers. 'The walls come together and crush whatever is between them.'

'What sets them off?' Magda waved to the far side of the hall. 'How do we get past?'

Bernger studied the distance between the landing and where the splinters were pressed into the wall. 'Roald must have held the pole out from here to try and trigger the mechanism.' He sighed and took a firm grip on what was left of the pole. Careful to keep every part of his own body on the landing, he thrust it into the corridor.

They waited in tense silence as seconds passed without any result. Bernger could hear his own heart pounding as he braced himself for a reaction. When it came, it did so with alarming abruptness. The walls smashed together, crushing the end of the pole between them. Bernger stumbled back, his hands locked on the further-shortened stump of splintered wood.

'How can we possibly get past that?' Magda cried out.

'I think I know how it works now,' Bernger said. He hesitated before telling her his idea. He wanted to make sure. 'We'll try it again. Start counting when I throw the pole into the room.'

Magda nodded. She started as soon as he made his throw. 'One... two... three...' The pole clattered to the floor almost three quarters of the way into the room. '... eight... nine... ten...' At thirteen she stopped counting. The walls came crashing together and pulverised what was left of the pole.

'A count of thirteen,' Bernger stated. 'That's how long we have to get from here to there. This trap operates on time. The mechanism starts as soon as something's between the walls. After a specific interval, it crushes–'

'Don't,' Magda said. 'It's enough to imagine it. I don't need you to tell me.'

Bernger nodded. He removed Klueger's book and tore out a page. He scrawled a message to the witch hunter, describing how he thought the trap worked and how to get past it. At the end of the missive, he advised him that if he saw remains in the hall, it meant Bernger was wrong.

'We'll have to run.' Magda shook her head. 'Only to a count of thirteen... I don't know if it's possible.'

'I can go across first,' Bernger offered. 'If I'm wrong... If I don't make it, you can figure something else out.'

'No,' Magda said. She glanced down at the bloodstains on the floor. 'I'm not going to stay down here alone. Besides, if I had to watch you... I'd never have the nerve to try by myself.'

'Together then,' Bernger said. He took Magda's hand and held it tight. 'When we move, start the count.' He took a deep breath, nerving himself for the ordeal ahead.

Then they were off. Racing for their lives against the sinister machinery. The count Magda kept sounded like a funeral bell in Bernger's ears. Each number was that much closer to a horrible death.

They reached the opposite landing at a count of eleven. Bernger collapsed as he lunged out from the trapped room. Magda reeled and fell across him. They heard the ferocious smack of the walls slamming together behind them.

Magda started to laugh. Raucous, jubilant laughter. The thrill of survival when death had seemed assured. Bernger joined in, venting all the nervous tension that coursed through him.

'We made it! By Ranald, we made it!' Bernger rapped his knuckles three times against the floor to thank the trickster god for their good fortune.

It was many minutes before they were composed enough to continue. Bernger walked around the corner of the landing. He stopped short when he saw what lay ahead of them. There was a kind of natural cavern illuminated by some phosphorescent crystal growth that peppered the rock walls. A stout door of iron stood out from one of the walls. It was the first door they'd seen since entering the dungeon.

'Could that be the way out?' Magda waved at the door.

'I think it is,' Bernger said gravely. When Magda gave him a curious stare, he directed her attention away from the door and to something much closer.

Yawning almost at their very feet was a deep pit. Glowing crystals littered its walls, casting the depths in light. Slithering at the bottom of the hole were dozens of long, sinuous, copper-scaled creatures.

'Ore-adders,' Bernger said. 'They feed on metal, but that doesn't mean they won't spray venom at us if we disturb them.' He pointed out the thin, narrow planks that crossed the pit. Each had long chains dangling from them into the hole, low enough that their motion was sure to be noticed by the serpents.

'That's the trap then,' Magda groaned. 'Try to cross the pit and the snakes spit poison on you. Freedom's just the other side, but it's impossible to cross.'

'No,' Bernger said. 'There's a way across. We just have to figure out what it is.'

Bernger hoped his words sounded more confident than they felt.

Klueger poured the essential salts from the sigmarite flask. The azure powder had a faint glow to it, an aura from the Celestial Realm. It was ground down from the shed skins of stardrakes by the Sacrosanct Chambers of the Stormcast Eternals. Some among the Order of Azyr were granted the privilege of carrying these dragon castings, and Klueger had been blessed to be deemed worthy of such a charge. He had only used a few pinches of the powder before, against the daemons he had encountered in the past. That had been enough to restrict and bind such lowly manifestations of Chaos. It would take much more to defy a fiend like the Mardagg.

Lothar paced about the trophy room, his robes swirling around him in his agitation. 'A pentacle,' he repeated as he observed Klueger's work. 'The shape can both attract and bind the daemon.'

The alchemist's words reeked of corruption and forbidden knowledge. Klueger felt ashamed to pay them any heed. Yet now he was attending Lothar's instructions as though they were spoken by Grand Lector Sieghard.

'There's no need to attract the Mardagg,' Klueger reminded him. 'We already have what it wants.' It was a petty thing to say, but he enjoyed the way the alchemist trembled.

'Leave an opening,' Lothar said when he had recovered enough to speak. 'By all the gods, do not forget to leave a place for it to enter!'

'A fine one to speak of the gods, since you've flaunted their authority.' Klueger pressed the ivory stopper back in the flask and stepped out from the pentacle. There was a gap between the points that faced the doorway. 'You can have faith in this much – I'll seal the pentacle if it steps inside. I'll also pray it's strong enough to hold the daemon.'

Lothar eyed the door that led down to the dungeon. It wasn't the first time he'd done so. Klueger knew he was evaluating his chances against the traps. Whether he was better risking them or the daemon. The witch hunter tapped his pistol against one of the display cases. 'Here I'll defend you,' he said. 'I gave my word. Go down there and you are on your own.'

The alchemist started to say something, but he choked on the words. His eyes widened in terror. He stared towards the doorway and the dark corridor beyond. Klueger couldn't see anything, but he knew wizards were more attuned to the occult than men who practised less unsavoury vocations. Soon, the carnage-ridden reek of the daemon wafted into the room. A few moments more and he heard the ghoulish sounds of dripping blood and naked feet.

Klueger swung around and hurried to the spot he'd chosen to hide himself, a row of armour that flanked the pentacle. There was no point in Lothar trying to hide. The Mardagg would sense him anyway. The alchemist stood several feet from the top of the pentacle and faced his approaching doom.

The stench of blood preceded the daemon, rolling into the room and making it stink like an abattoir. A long, bony hand gripped the edge of the doorway, the claws scratching against the iron setting. Then the Mardagg stalked inwards. The once splendid clothes Thilo had worn were now gore-soaked rags. The daemon had expanded, stretched and twisted the youth's body until it was twice its original size. The fangs that protruded from its skull were like glistening daggers. The boiling pools of blood that filled its sockets shone with an infernal light.

The first few steps it took, the daemon exhibited some degree of caution. Its head swung back and forth, searching the room for ambush. Before it did more than glance at Klueger's hiding spot, the Mardagg growled and locked its hellish gaze upon Lothar. A wolfish snarl rattled through the skeletal daemon. It lunged forwards, intent upon its prey.

Incomplete, the pentacle was nothing but dust on the floor to a daemon of such profane might as the Mardagg. It wouldn't stop the fiend. Klueger sprang from hiding and threw himself across the floor. He had the last of the essential salts clenched in both fists. Crying out the name of Dracothion, he slammed both hands down and closed the figure.

The Mardagg roared when it realised what was happening. It leapt for Lothar, but the pentacle had been completed in time. As it rushed for the alchemist, a sheet of blue lightning crackled around its crimson body. The gangrel daemon snarled in pain as it retreated from the barrier. It swiped its claws in Lothar's direction, only to be thwarted by another burst of electricity.

'It won't die!' Lothar screamed. 'It isn't going to die!'

Klueger had seen the dragon castings reduce lesser daemons to nothingness instantly. The Mardagg, while hurt by the barrier, wasn't destroyed. In fact, it didn't even seem to be wounded, only provoked. It lunged again at the barrier and struggled to push its way through.

'It *will* die,' Klueger vowed. He drew his pistol and fired into the fiend. The sigmarite bullets weren't affected by the pentacle's barrier. They passed through to crack against the Mardagg's ribs, shattering three of them. The daemon staggered, its skull pressing against the warding field and causing its head to be enveloped in blue electricity. The monster howled, but didn't fall. Instead it pressed against the edge of the pentacle, trying to overwhelm the barrier.

'It won't die!' Lothar's terrified wail echoed through the trophy room.

Klueger cast aside the spent pistol and whipped his silvered sword from its sheath. He dashed around the pentacle. Even he was starting to wonder if it would hold the Mardagg. If the daemon broke through, he was determined that it would need to get through him to reach Lothar. Alive, the alchemist ensured the daemon could not leave its current host. The murderous spirit was trapped in a cage of flesh.

The witch hunter's blade slashed through the barrier and raked the daemon's arm. Foul ichor sprayed from the wound. It sizzled and steamed as it struck the warding field. Klueger swung again and broke two more of the exposed ribs. The Mardagg swatted at him in retaliation, but its claws were thrown back by a burst of electricity. Klueger could attack across the pentacle. The daemon couldn't.

Then the Mardagg drew back. Its arms fell to its sides. The daemon fixed Klueger with its hideous gaze. He could feel its hate pressing down on him, but there was something more. There was a sardonic humour in that look. The mocking contempt born from only the bitterest enmity.

The skeletal body rapidly began to decay. Strands of flesh turned to crimson slime. Blood gushed from corroded organs. Bones cracked and splintered, striking the floor as little more than shards. The skull fell in upon itself, the glowing eyes bursting in a shower of gore. In only a matter of moments, the giant daemon was nothing but a heap of putrid slush.

Klueger felt cold inside as he watched the daemon's dissolution. He knew this was no victory. This wasn't the work of the barrier or his sword.

The witch hunter slowly turned around. He saw Lothar's lifeless body on the ground. His face was discoloured, almost black, and there was a greenish spittle dripping from his lips. In his hand was a bottle. Certain that the Mardagg would break through the barrier, the alchemist had decided to cheat the daemon by taking poison.

Klueger shook his head. The daemon was free now, no longer held by either a magic pentacle or a cage of flesh.

Magda stared down at the copper-coloured reptiles. The serpents crawled about the walls of the pit. There were what looked like iron circles embedded into the circumference. As she watched, one of the ore-adders stopped in front of a metal disc. Its hood snapped open, and from its fangs it spit a stream of burning venom onto the iron. It bubbled, and a molten ooze dribbled away from the circle. The snake dipped its head and started to drink the liquid sludge.

'So that's how the snakes sustain themselves,' Magda said.

Bernger followed the direction of her gaze. 'Before he put them down there, Alrik must have lined the pit with iron rods.' He pointed to several dark holes that had the same dimensions as the metal circles. 'Ore-adders will follow a vein until it has been played out. They don't need to eat too often, so a single twenty-foot-long rod might feed them for a year.'

'Is there a way to use that to help us?' Magda wondered. She turned her gaze to the planks that stretched over the pit and the chains hanging from them. 'Why don't they eat the chains?'

'Forged metal is indigestible to them,' Bernger said. 'Their venom can dissolve raw ore but not anything that has been fired in a forge.' He studied the planks and the serpents below. He held his hand out to Magda. 'Hold on to me and pull me back if this is a mistake. I want to try something.'

Magda took a firm grip on Bernger's hand. She didn't know

what he was going to do, but it was clear they had to try something. Knowing that salvation might be so close was torture. Especially when any moment might have the daemon seeping into her body. Consuming her soul.

But the Mardagg did have its own things to offer. The power of revenge.

Magda's fingers tightened on Bernger's hand. He spun around, anxiety on his face.

'What's wrong?'

'Nothing,' Magda said. 'Just nervous.' She didn't know how to explain the strange thought that had flashed through her mind. The horrible realisation that there was some part of her that wanted to submit to the Mardagg and let the daemon take over. With salvation so close, how could she possibly resist the prospect of escape?

Bernger set his foot out on the plank. As he pressed his weight down, it began to tip upwards from a pivot ten feet further along. The chains fixed to the bottom rattled against the floor of the pit. Agitated snakes reared back and spat venom up towards the plank. Magda pulled as Bernger shifted back to the landing before any of the poison could land on him.

'Well, that explains how it works, anyway,' Bernger said. He tried to put confidence in his tone, but Magda could tell he was rattled by the experience. With his weight withdrawn, the plank tilted back to its former position.

'We'd have to move fast,' Magda said. 'Too fast to be cautious.'

'Thirty feet at a run,' Bernger said. 'Keep your balance or visit the snakes.' He looked down into the pit. The ore-adders had quieted down when the chains stopped moving around them. Venom dripped from the plank. The serpents weren't accurate at any distance. 'Get unlucky, even a little of that poison on your skin, and you'll go mad with pain. You'll fall before you even know what's happening.'

'There has to be a way,' Magda said. She saw that Bernger was surprised by the ferocity in her tone. He'd be even more stunned if he knew why. The insane urge to stay in the castle was nagging at her. To reject its influence, Magda had to focus, had to compel discipline. All the concentration Ottokar had demanded from her when she practised with the sword. Now she needed that intensity of thought to bring her through the dungeon.

Bernger was silent for a moment, watching the venom dripping off the chains. 'They will attack anything that disturbs them. There's no way to rush across those planks without making the chains move.' He plucked at his coat and pointed at Magda's clothes. 'This isn't thick enough to keep the venom from seeping through to our skin.'

Magda nodded. She reached into a pouch hanging from her belt and removed a silver coin. 'What if we give the snakes something else to annoy them?' She threw the coin down into the pit. The ore-adders near where it landed started spitting at it.

'Too much to hope their venom will hurt the other snakes,' Bernger said. 'Their scales are too thick. And the coin doesn't move around long enough to hold their attention. Not long enough to do us any good, at least.'

Silence lingered between them. Magda gave the pit closer scrutiny. Finally she noticed something odd. None of the snakes crawled near a particular spot. She saw why. There was an ugly stain there that had a vaguely serpentine shape. 'What do you think that is?'

Bernger stared at it for a moment. 'It looks like a dead ore-adder. They decay pretty fast.'

'The other snakes don't seem interested in going near it,' Magda observed. 'In fact, they seem to abhor getting anywhere close to it.'

Bernger considered that point for a moment. Eventually he shook his head. 'Maybe they just don't like to be near their own dead. I don't know how that can help us. It's not like we can go down there and get it.'

'Then we try something else,' Magda said. She removed Ottokar's sword and drew it out of the scabbard. 'You have a knife?'

Bernger gave her a puzzled look. 'What do you have in mind?' he asked as he removed the blade from inside his boot and proffered it to her.

'If we can't go down to the snakes, maybe we can bring them up to us.' She removed her jacket and took the knife. Quickly she began to cut the garment into long strips. She waved her hand at Bernger. 'I think we'll need your coat as well.'

Bernger was confused as he handed it over to her. 'I don't–'

'It's simple. We need a cord long enough to reach down into the pit,' Magda said. 'Unless you're sneaking a coil of rope around with you, we have to make do. I'll cut these into strips, bind them together, and we'll have something long enough to go into the pit.'

'What good will that do?'

Magda set her hand against Ottokar's sword. 'Not everything my father taught me about fighting was entirely honourable,' she said. 'He showed me a unique way to deal with someone who is better than me. They couldn't be wearing armour if it was to work, but I don't think these snakes are going to suddenly start putting on steel plate.'

The last was meant as a jest, but there was no humour in her tone. Tension raced through her body. She hoped Bernger wouldn't notice how firmly she gripped the knife. She prayed he had no idea that her mind was boiling with ghastly images and the insane desire to see his blood spraying across the walls.

Magda crouched down beside the coat. She stabbed the knife into it and began to cut. 'I'll throw the strips to you. Tie them into a cord.'

'And then?'

'Then I'm going to try to spear one of those snakes and see if we can get across this pit,' Magda said. The words were meant more for herself than for him. The urge to stay behind was getting stronger with every heartbeat.

It took some time before the cord was long enough to suit Magda's purpose. While Bernger wrote down their plan and left it for Klueger and Inge to read, she busied herself with the last part of her idea. One end of the cord was tied firmly around the hilt of Ottokar's sword, the other secured to the scabbard. Another strip of cloth fastened the scabbard to her arm. She held the sword against her chest. As a little girl she'd always been confident that her father's sword would be there to protect her. Never could she have dreamed it would be in such an unusual way.

'Are you ready?' Bernger asked.

Magda didn't say anything, just gave the slightest nod. She fought to focus, to blot out the destructive impulse to stay behind.

Fixating upon one of the snakes, Magda braced herself for the effort ahead. She waited and watched, biding her time until everything was perfect before she made her cast. The sword flew down into the pit like a javelin. Its point impaled one of the snakes. The reptile writhed on the blade while those around it spun around and started spitting venom at the sword. True to Bernger's words, the acid did no harm to the forged steel.

'Help me pull it back,' Magda said. In striking the snake, the sword had embedded itself in the floor. It took both of them to free it. They carefully began to draw the cord back. Every second they thought the impaled snake would slide off the blade, but their dread wasn't realised. More, Magda could see the other snakes frantically crawling away from the transfixed reptile.

'Something's happening to them,' Bernger called out. He pointed, and Magda could see that several of the snakes were twitching in pain.

'Be ready to grab the snake when I pull it up,' Magda said. Both of them had wound strips of cloth about their hands. She hoped it was enough to let them safely handle the dying reptile.

The hanging sword slowly came up over the edge of the pit. Bernger leaned down to grab the snake. Magda saw the spray of venom that flew past his ear as the wounded ore-adder reacted. Before it could strike again, Bernger had his hand around its neck. Grimly, he pulled the writhing body off the blade.

Magda scowled at the damage inflicted on her father's sword. The blade was pitted and scarred where it had struck the snake, eaten away as though by a powerful acid. 'I thought you said the venom couldn't hurt forged metal.'

'It can't,' Bernger said. He held the snake out at arm's length. They could see a ghastly slime bubbling from the serpent's wound. The ore-adder's scales steamed and blistered wherever the liquid dripped.

Magda understood at once. Her throw had punctured the snake's belly, and now it was leaking digestive juices, stomach acids powerful enough to eat through the metal meals the snakes consumed. Although safe within the stomach, the juices were even more caustic than their venom when the snake's belly was ruptured. That was why they so assiduously avoided a decaying ore-adder, lest the leaking acids kill them as well.

'We have a way to fight back,' Magda said. She held the sword out to Bernger. 'Put the snake back on the blade and tie it fast. We'll give the ones in the pit something worse to worry about than those chains.'

Magda led the way across the plank. She waved the sword from side to side as she moved, spattering drops from the dead serpent down onto the heads of its fellows. Each step she took created pandemonium among the reptiles. The snakes ignored the swaying chains, instead writhing away in panic as the acid dripped down onto them.

Bernger followed Magda, plunging after her across the planks. They tipped and swayed, threatening to send the survivors tumbling at every step. Her mind afire with concentrating upon her footing and keeping the snakes distracted, Magda didn't need the added complaint of the urge to turn back and return to the castle. Only a few feet from the other side, her foot slipped. She stared down into the crawling pit and felt death rushing up at her.

Instead she was tackled from behind and sent sprawling. The cord tied to her arm broke as it was raked across the edge of the pit. Strangely, it was the loss of Ottokar's sword that wracked her thoughts more than the closeness of her escape.

Bernger rose from the floor, his face aglow with victory. He held his fists in the air and shouted, roaring like a bloodreaver with a mound of victims heaped beneath his boots. Magda blinked in fright at the weird analogy and the vile picture it conjured in her mind. The vivid horror of atrocity and its obscene appeal.

'We made it!' Bernger crowed as he reached to help Magda to her feet. 'I'm sorry if I hurt you, but we made it! We're across!'

Magda tried to make sense of what he was saying. Was there cause to celebrate? She glanced back at the pit. Yes, it was him. He'd grabbed her when she was going to fall. Why had he done that?

Bernger turned away and hurried to the door. He was excited, but not too excited to cast aside all caution. He examined the portal carefully, studying it for any sign of more traps. 'I can smell fresh air,' he called out. 'Once we have this open, we can escape the castle.'

Escape the castle? Magda shook her head. That wasn't what she wanted. Or was it? Something inside her kept saying she had something important to do in Mhurghast. Something it would help her do.

'Are you all right?' Bernger asked when he looked towards Magda. 'Did you get hurt?'

Magda wanted to shout. She wanted to warn him. She wanted to tell him to run, to throw open that door and flee. Flee for his life. Flee for his soul. She wanted to do that. But she also wanted to open his belly and watch his blood spill across the floor. She wanted to take his head and carve upon it the Skull Rune and lay it down before the Brass Throne.

There was worry and concern in Bernger's eyes. He laid his hand on her shoulder. 'Are you all right?' he asked again.

Shock filled his face as Magda drove Bernger's own knife into his stomach. She twisted and ripped, tearing through flesh and organs. Strength such as she'd never known pulsated down her arm, into her hand, through her fingers. The knife was no longer a knife – it was sacred. An instrument of the Blood God to nurture His insatiable thirst.

There was no regret in Magda's mind when she watched Bernger stagger away. Only numb indifference as he stumbled to the edge of the snake pit. She didn't react when he fell in. He didn't matter – he was nothing. He had no part in what she wanted to do. What she needed to do.

Revenge, the thing clawing at the foundations of her soul

howled to her. It was slipping away even as it tried to tighten its hold. The chain was broken. It couldn't linger. Not unless she said it could.

Revenge, the Mardagg hissed, and in its whisper it told Magda why. Why she had to go back into the castle.

Why she needed revenge.

EPILOGUE

Klueger made his way through Mhurghast's dungeon. Every room he entered, he did so with a feeling of dread. Would this be the place where he would find Magda, killed by some murderous device? How far had Bernger managed to lead her? How great was the extent of these deathly halls?

There could be no other escape now. Klueger had realised that the moment the daemon abandoned Thilo's body. He had no proof of the Mardagg's destruction that he could offer that would satisfy Grand Lector Sieghard. The castle would burn, along with all inside it. The only chance for life was the escape route guarded by the count's traps.

When he saw that the body of Baron von Woernhoer and the decayed husk of his killer had been moved, Klueger's anxiety swelled. Bernger and Magda had got this far. That was to be expected, since they knew the secret of the other rooms. What lay ahead of them would be the unknown. A deadly unknown.

Klueger slowly rounded the corner to the other part of the landing. He found the note left by Bernger. His eyes roved across the pencilled words and their final warning. He looked across the fifth chamber, but to his relief there wasn't any trace of pulped bodies, only the splinters from the pole. Bernger had been right, then. He and Magda had won clear of this trap at least.

The witch hunter sprinted across the trapped corridor, calling out numbers as he ran. He reached the other side only a few seconds before the walls crashed together behind him. Their dolorous reverberation pounded through his ears. It was why he didn't hear the footsteps that approached him from around the corner that led to the next room.

'I knew I would find you,' Magda called. He looked up to see her walking towards him. The expression on her face was cold, vacant. Only the eyes were vibrant. Klueger could see the rage smouldering in them.

'Praise Sigmar you're safe!' he cried out, relief flooding through him. But even as he said the words, he knew something was wrong. There was a smell. A charnel reek that grew in intensity.

'No one is safe,' Magda said. As she spoke, her voice began to collapse inwards, deepening into a bestial snarl that reverberated not in Klueger's ears but in the depths of his soul.

'She gave herself to me, that I might thank you on behalf of her mother,' rasped the Mardagg's voice inside Klueger's spirit.

The enraged eyes turned bright crimson as tears of blood spilled down Magda's cheeks. The Mardagg raised one of her hands and reached out for Klueger. The pale skin cracked, blood spurting from torn veins as the fingers lengthened into bony claws.

'Revenge.' The word echoed through the dungeons of Mhurghast long after the witch hunter's screams fell into silence.

ABOUT THE AUTHOR

C L Werner's Black Library credits include the Age of Sigmar novels *Overlords of the Iron Dragon, The Tainted Heart* and *Beastgrave*, the novella 'Scion of the Storm' in *Hammers of Sigmar*, the Warhammer novels *Deathblade, Mathias Thulmann: Witch Hunter, Runefang* and *Brunner the Bounty Hunter*, the Thanquol and Boneripper series and Time of Legends: The Black Plague series. For Warhammer 40,000 he has written the Space Marine Battles novel *The Siege of Castellax*. Currently living in the American south-west, he continues to write stories of mayhem and madness set in the Warhammer worlds.

YOUR NEXT READ

WARHAMMER HORROR

THE HOUSE OF NIGHT AND CHAIN
by David Annandale

At the edge of the city of Valgaast, Malveil awaits. It is a house of darkness, its halls filled with history and pain. It knows all secrets, and no weakness can escape its insidious gaze. Now it stirs eagerly at the approach of prey.

Available from **blacklibrary.com, games-workshop.com, Games Workshop** and **Warhammer** stores, all good book stores or visit one of the thousands of independent retailers worldwide, which can be found at **games-workshop.com/storefinder**